THE
LIGHT
OF A
CUBAN
SON

THE
LIGHT
OF A
CUBAN
SON

LORENZO CHAVEZ

Light Messages
Torchflame Books
Durham, NC

The Light of a Cuban Son
Lorenzo Chavez
lorenzochavezauthor.com

Published 2022, by Torchflame Books
an Imprint of Light Messages Publishing
www.lightmessages.com
Durham, NC 27713 USA
SAN: 920-9298

Paperback ISBN: 978-1-61153-435-1
E-book ISBN: 978-1-61153-436-8
Library of Congress Control Number: 2022904685

For everyone I have ever known.

The Untold Want

The untold want by life and land ne'er granted,
Now voyager sail thou forth to seek and find.

—Walt Whitman

A Note from the Author

I wanted to tell a story about a gay child growing up in a culture that believed keeping secrets was the socially acceptable thing to do, and where child abuse and mental illness were never acknowledged or discussed.

I wanted to explore cause and effect, and to show how traumatic events in a child's life linger on to resurface once and again. This required the story to move between the child's most intimate thoughts and a wider, more panoramic view of his world. This required the narrative to show how the bewildered child makes the wrong decision at nearly every turn.

While much of what happens in this novel is based on my own life experience, I understood from the beginning that a memoir could never fully convey what I wanted to express in the way a novel could. The characters I created exist to support the narrative arch; they do not represent an individual. Rather, they represent the depth and breadth of the Cuban society I remember from my early life.

Likewise, places have been left undefined to prevent the realities of the physical world from rooting the reader to a particular locale. I wanted readers to visualize a universe that is only bound by the limits of their imagination.

To be sure, some of the scenes in this novel will be difficult to read, but this first-person narrative works to illustrate what the young boy sees and feels, describing specific situations in the limited language of a child.

An eight-year-old does not know the meaning of assault, and this novel should never be interpreted as an endorsement of child abuse. To the contrary, I wanted to show all the damage that such adult actions and the ensuing silence, ignorance, and denial have on a child.

I also wanted to show how a young man of seventeen was able to use all his experiences to navigate through his own trauma and become a functioning adult.

I wanted the reader to walk away believing in determination and hope. I wanted to share my belief that though life is never perfect, it is indeed possible to step into the void, to endure it, and to survive.

This is not a story about one boy's life, but a story about ten, one hundred, a thousand, a million boys' lives.

A New Soul

Mother's slow labor allowed enough time for the provincial hospital to send a telegram and for Father to come in from the fields, wash up, get dressed, and undertake the two-hour journey to be present for my birth. He wore the same cream linen suit, heavily starched white cotton shirt, red and yellow tie, two-tone shoes, and Panama-style hat that he had worn on the first day he visited my maternal grandparents' prosperous farm. On that day, he arrived determined to ask for Mother's hand after meeting her just once at a dance.

Twenty-four hours from the start of her contractions, after enduring the trauma of a difficult delivery that was to leave her forever unable to conceive, a blue baby boy in need of life support was rushed into an incubator. It was the early hours of St. Valentine's Day of 1954. This was my birth. My name is Martín Cruz.

Father was taken to see me through the separating glass wall, and his normally expressionless face became rigid and tense, his lips reduced to an invisible slit. He offered no comments, nor did he ask any questions, insisting instead to be taken to Mother at once.

There were no rooms in the maternity ward, and the curtains separating her bed from the common hallway were only partly closed.

Father offered her no congratulating words, nor did he ask how she was or how she felt. Instead, he focused on the tall window at the far wall. After inhaling deeply, he finally

spoke: "*Ese niño es muy prieto. ¿Con qué negro te acostaste?*"
Noticing that I was very dark, he wanted to know which
black man she'd had sex with. He walked out, not waiting to
hear her answer, leaving Mother and me behind and alone.

Mother would spend her entire life reliving the memory
of her labor injuries and the moment when his adulterous
accusations were made—each new recollection building
upon the earlier recollections to become more traumatic
than the last.

In my life, there has never been a moment when I wasn't
aware of these stories, and hearing them as a young child
always left me confused. I believed that the anger and the
fights were because of me. That the *amargura* that Mother
harbored was because of me. That my imperfect birth was
the reason for everything bad that happened in our house.
This is the earliest burden I took on.

FIRST GIFT

I recovered to become a pale pink baby, and when Father arrived three weeks later to take us back to the family farm, after seeing me once again, he no longer doubted that I was his son.

Some of the women had heard his comments on the morning of my birth, and by the time of his return, everyone at the hospital was aware of what he had said. But that morning, they all behaved as if nothing had happened. Instead, they showered him with congratulations and well wishes on the birth of his son. Feeling rejected and ignored, Mother smiled and had little to say.

Through the journey back to her parent's farm where they had made their home, she could not find a way to confront him about his behavior right after my birth. Once home, Father was happy returning to his repetitive days and nights at the farm. Mother used the anger she felt as the fuel to power her day. She cried as I cried.

My maternal grandfather, whom we all called Papá, knew his daughter very well, and he knew that something was wrong, but could not get an answer from her. Mother was convinced that if she repeated Father's words even once, the fragile world she had built—and perhaps even her life— would end.

In the unspoken chaos, I became unable to keep down any food or thrive. Cow's milk, sheep milk, and even mare's milk was tried, but my colic and vomiting never stopped.

Midwives and then the doctor were sent for, but none were able to offer any hope. Everyone became convinced that I would be the next child to die at the farm.

Papá reacted by sending Father on the four-hour trip to the capital, with instructions for him to find work, to find a place to live where Mother could make a home of her own, and to find a doctor who'd help me survive.

He returned three weeks later with good news, and a journey was planned. Papá paying for this move was his first gift to me. In time, he was to grant me many more.

EXPEDITION

Our pilgrimage to Havana on that November Sunday of 1954, when I was nine months old, had become a dream innocently fabricated out of spun sugar and meringue, delicate and fragile, and neatly wrapped in hope. Not hope in God's intervention, but hopes tied together with the ribbons of imagined good fortunes and unspoken dreams that were still to come.

Mother, Father, Mother's younger sister Cecilia, and me. My family on that day was no more than a band of country people used to the affluence and social status they had enjoyed at the family's farm.

These adults were a trio of naive well-off farmers who spoke in the round melodic voices of the countryside, each proudly flashing their one shiny gold-capped tooth with every smile, unaware that such an ornament was to brand them as backward and uneducated in the eyes of the social-climbing classes waiting for them. For Mother, the pain of these rejections was yet unknown.

ADVENT

The bus pulled into the capital in the late afternoon, just as the sun began to bleed orange and purple into the sky. It had been a good trip, and unconsciously everyone took the place that they'd repeatedly take during all future trips back to the farm. Father, the man, sat up front, while the women sat right behind him in the next row. By the window, Mother was calm, almost serene, and I, reacting to the quietness, had relaxed, kept down some food, and slept for much of the ride. Father's cousin Benita and her husband, Celestino, were there to greet us. In that triumphant moment, past injuries didn't seem to matter as much.

Benita was a round and expressive woman with prominent cheeks, a continuous smile, and a tendency to reach out with both arms to hug you a little too tight and a little too long, as if by loving you she was taking away all your hurt. She always wanted to squeeze me and kiss me. I still remember the wetness of her kisses on my face, which I was always quick to wipe away as she pretended not to notice, choosing instead to giggle at my silly fidgeting. I do not think it was possible for her to feel offended by anything anyone did or said.

Her wavy black hair flowed down her back, and her intense brown eyes were familiar to me. They were my eyes, my father's eyes, my paternal grandmother's eyes—Abuela's eyes. Her skin was a deep olive tan, but not in the way of a mulata, or in the way a woman of Taíno Indian blood is a dark tan. She was dark in the way the southern Spanish Gitanas are dark.

Celestino wasn't anything like his wife. If she was shapely and round, he was thin and pliable as a willow branch. Not tall but wiry, with a long face, flat cheeks, pointed jaw, and the teeth of a horse, which clinched tightly to the cigar he was never without. His straight-across eyebrows served as a visor for his small moss-colored eyes, and his head was topped by thick, very tight, light-brown curls. He had exceptionally large fleshy ear lobes that sat flat and hung low at the sides of his face. I have never forgotten how they flapped about with each of his boisterous laughs. I remember Mother pointing out this imperfection—*¡Oye! Qué orejas tan grandes el tiene.* She called him *El Orejón.* He was a witty and unfussy man. Watching Benita and Celestino together in action was like watching a comedy act.

A taxi dropped us in front of the long alley where Benita and Celestino lived. Slowly, the group walked to the last apartment, which was small but neat and clean. Benita had dinner ready for us.

Speaking in a musical voice filled with love, she emphasized and stretched every word as to signal the sincerity and the happiness she felt by having us in her home, reminding everyone about the apartment she and Celestino had made ready for us:

"Miren, están es su casa. Quédense tranquilos. Nos quedamos esta noche con la hija, así que no se preocupen de nada. Ahí hay café y comida y cosas para el niño. Mañana los llevaremos a su nuevo apartamento, que es muy bonito y ya está todito arreglado para ustedes."

That night, Benita and Celestino stayed with their married daughter, Ada, down the block. She had recently given birth to a little girl named Sandra, a cousin who would become an intrinsic part of my early life, and whose memory will always bring joy to my heart. The next day, they'd take us to our own apartment and help us settle in.

Morning arrived with Benita and Celestino surprising the family with plump loaves of freshly baked Cuban bread, which is not as hard to chew as a French baguette, or as salty as Italian bread. This bread has a thin and crispy golden crust and a hot, fluffy white center. Eating only the inside while leaving the crust intact would become a habit that I have never been able to break.

Benita offered to feed me that morning so that the adults could enjoy their breakfast and prepare for the day ahead. As I contentedly drank warm milk sweetened with honey and vanilla, they gathered around the small dining table to drink scorching-hot *café con leche* and eat generous portions of the steamy bread drenched in *mantequilla, mermelada de guayaba, y felicidad*—butter, guava marmalade, and happiness.

A Simple Bowl

It is a curious thing that I always remember each of my childhood and adolescent homes by a particular dish. My memories of our first apartment in Havana run back to just before I turned three years old. Eating a heaping bowl of *ajiaco*—the basic Cuban stew consisting of many roots, chicken, and fresh rings of corn on the cob—always reminds me of those early years in that home.

That apartment was reached through a long and narrow cement alleyway on Calle D'Estrampes, near Calle San Miguel. Its front door opened directly into a small, square living room dressed in modest furnishings, with just a chair, a sofa, a side table, and no lamps. There was no television, but a radio broke the silence by playing popular *guajiro* country songs. No pictures adorned the walls, and the only decoration was a small cream-colored vase with slight earlobes holding four red plastic roses that contrasted against the pale-green walls. Next to it, a mother-of-pearl frame displayed my parents' wedding portrait.

A dim light bulb hanging from a simple plaster medallion in the center of the ceiling washed the room in a golden glow. This light didn't reach the corners of the room, and I was always trying to make friends with the shadows as they tried to free themselves from the walls.

During the day, broken light came through the front iron-barred window to brighten Mother's long hours at the sewing machine, which rested below. However, I never picture myself there with her as a three-year-old; the kitchen at the other end of the house was my home.

In my yellow kitchen kingdom lived a deep-brown wooden table supported by a pedestal in the shape of a chalice that stood on four legs forming the shape of a cross. These wide legs were flat, and I could easily sit upon them in comfort for hours, happily alone in my fantasy world. In there, the black leather bottoms of the rigid studded Colonial-style chairs were my easel, my blank sheets of paper my canvas, my coloring pencils my paint and brush. There, I painted borderless orange, yellow, green, and blue balloons floating away into a clear, happy sky.

Not too far from the table, a white sink sat under another barred window, and beyond it, I could see the top of a tall brick wall where nimble pigeons romanced one another from morning until dusk. Once a week, Mother hung Father's just-washed work shirts on the clothesline, blocking the happy lovers from view with their long sleeves as they reached up in a prayer to the sun.

At the far wall of the room, a small gas tabletop stove sat on a white metal cart. A white refrigerator stood to the left, and at night it was always in repose, its enormous silver handle reflecting the flickering round florescent light above. But during the day, when invoked, this handle opened the door to shockingly display its turquoise inner walls.

Every night, once the evening meal had been completed and the dishes had been stored, a small cot was unfolded in front of the sink to become my bed, crushing the table and chairs against the opposite wall.

There, all alone in the dark, I eagerly waited for those nights when the passion of the moon traveled in the sky to visit me so I'd no longer be alone. During those nights, the moon's light caressed my small size with its silvery robes to become the magic shield that even today I treasure and love.

ADMISSIONS

Mother worked from home, embroidering appliques for a nearby sweatshop. New work arrived every morning and left every night. Six days a week, each new day always the same as the last.

Late in her old age, after life had robbed her of the skill to hide her emotions, Mother admitted to me that in those days she felt unfocused, unwanted, left behind. I didn't respond.

There were a few minutes of silence, and then she spoke through tears to tell me that Father had only married her because she had ridiculed him once at a dance.

Quickly then, the cadence of her voice changing from bitterness to scorn, she told me that in that period of her life at our first home, working in isolation while caring for me felt like a punishment which she didn't deserve.

After holding her breath and changing her mood to reflect the hatred in her eyes, Mother admitted to me that she and Father were at their happiest before I was born.

Was it anger, rage, or pride that stopped me from crying or showing the devastation and rejection I felt? How could I not be, hearing at last the words behind the emotion that I had seen flash across her face all my life?

I got up from the table without speaking a word. I walked down the urine-scented hall, only stopping once to tell the nursing home staff that I would not be returning. I made it as far as the parking lot when pity for the old woman gained a foothold and I turned back because I understood that her mind was no longer her own.

Sitting in front of her once again, I reminded her of the times when she made sure that my shoes were clean and efficiently laced, and the times when she painstakingly arranged the curls in my hair after drenching each one in sweet violet water. Then, for a happy second, we both remembered the scent.

I chose to lie and not tell her that what I remembered the most from those days were her robotic actions and how they were lacking in warmth. Speaking those words would not have erased my newly discovered truth that her overwhelming confusion from those days had embroidered itself onto me and guided me for so much of my life.

THE HAND OF GOD

It was a cloudy late-January day and Mother had been busy preparing lunch. As usual, she had placed me on top of the kitchen table, and I contently watched her as she sliced and then dropped ripe plantains into the frying pan.

At one point, the flickering from the ceiling light reflected against the large knife sitting next to me in such a way as to frighten me because it made me recall that forgotten day when I reached for its shiny blade and sliced my left hand.

Unexpectedly, Mother turned away from the stove, slumped over the table and grasped the edge. Motionless, I watched her rigid body as she focused her gaze straight ahead as if wanting to break through the wall. I watched until I lost sight of her face and began to choke on the dense cloud from the lard burning on the stove. It was then that Father appeared in the kitchen and the frightening silence finally broke.

I watched as he turned off the stove and flung open the shuttered window with a bang to allow the smoke to escape, and then I took a breath, followed by many more breaths, while reaching for his arms. But he didn't come to my rescue, and instead focused his reproaching stares on her. They stared at each other until he spoke just one word: *¡Mujer!*

No other words were exchanged as Father walked out of the kitchen. I cried. Then Mother began screaming at me, shaking me, and demanding that I be quiet.

I cried as Mother screamed until a bright light broke through the clouds, rushing across the room and bleaching the drabness from the walls. Then everything paused and Mother became gentle and calm.

Embraced by the light, Mother held me close, and I grew safe and warm next to her, feeling the gift of her love.

PASSAGE

I regret that as a child I didn't see the importance of asking questions about my family's ancestral homes. I didn't ask about the voyages they took from Spain, or the struggles they overcame to create the world into which I was born. It has taken me most of my adult life to gather the few stories that I now know as facts. For I know now with near certainty about their crossings from unnamed places in Andalucía, Asturias, Las Canarias, and Galicia, into the Cuban countryside. There is so much more that I do not know.

Were they peasants working on another man's fields or the tradespeople of their town? Did they migrate to escape poverty, or were their pockets filled with gold? Did they live near the sea, and was it easy for them to find a ship to board? Or was their journey to the sea long and filled with imagined demons and perils? Were they unschooled and overwhelmed by things unknown, and by superstitions controlled? Did they believe only in themselves? Or did they believe for certain in a God they could trust? On their journeys, did they stop in the churches to pray or worship on the day set aside for the Lord?

I didn't think to ask these things when I had my family with me. And now, they are all gone.

BLOOD LINE

Everyone said that Mother's paternal grandfather, the man I only knew as Abuelito Agustín, had been fortunate in the possession of a proper last name—the kind of name that when spoken, confirmed its origins by the way that it was pronounced, all full of Zs and Qs. I remember the family saying that his speech declared that he spoke with a proper Castilian tongue—*Por supuesto que el era español. ¿No te acuerdas como hablaba?* This was enough to open doors for him not available to other men with lesser family names. But he was no longer young by the time I was born, and my remembrance of him is that of a small, wrinkled man who spoke in the quiet, raspy voice of age rather than a distinct accent that I could recognize.

Some said that he had inherited a large fortune and traveled to Cuba looking for land. Others claimed he was a soldier who fought for Spain, but then stayed behind at the end of the Spanish-American War. No one ever really knew how he arrived, but this didn't matter. In a country of so many immigrants with questionable pasts, it was best to never ask. He had the name, he had the land, and that was all that mattered back then.

Abuelita Elvira, Augustín's wife, as with so many people in the province where my family comes from, was born in the Canary Islands. She had reached Cuba with her two brothers and her parents as a small child of two years old, and held no memories from that life. Unlike her husband, she saw herself as a Cuban woman, not as an immigrant.

Her still-unwrinkled face was the color of a Saharan Bedouin; to me it seemed as if she had been caressed by the sun.

She was a tiny woman with ash-colored hair tightly bound in a small bun at the back of her head. An unassuming old woman who dressed in simple shades of tans and browns. A slight woman whose voice echoed the lilt of her heart. I loved Abuelita, and I find pride in believing that the small, faded image that sits by my bedside table today is the last known remaining image of her.

Something of Value

Though no one remembers when or how Abuelito Agustín took hold of the land, the stories I heard were of how much of it wasn't arable but wild, how the *Marabú* forests had conquered it long before he arrived.

Marabú is the predatory beast that ravages and devours the land if not fought back with blade and machine.

By the time of my earliest memories of the farm, much of this forest had been cut back, but I remember how the remaining twisted branches grew tall as a house. And I remember how painfully their long, piercing thorns perforated my feet, my arms, and my hands when I disobeyed the warnings and stepped into them—childishly, always imagining that I was a determined prince fighting to free Sleeping Beauty from her slumbering curse. And as for their lantern-shaped gold and purple flowers, I can still remember how far that scent traveled across the land.

Soon after I was born, *los abuelitos* Elvira and Augustin retired to the nearest affluent town when the farm was divided amongst Papá and his three younger brothers.

While each family clan lived within their own partition of the farm, they all contributed to the success of the whole enterprise.

There were sugar cane fields stretching as far away to where the land met the sky, but Papá alone—who held the largest plot of land—had groves where avocados, oranges, and guavas grew, which he then sold for a comfortable sum.

Through my child's eyes, it seemed as if they lived in harmony with one another and the land.

My strongest memory from those ideal days, when I was about six, is of the ancient black couple who traveled from farm to farm, looking for day work. I loved sitting with these two and listening to their charming stories about a life they probably never lived, but adventures I found so amazing that I could not help but tell them as my own time after time.

I remember my maternal grandmother—whom we called Mamá—inviting them to come in, sit at the table, and share our lunch whenever they passed by the house. I also remember how Papá so often granted them unlimited access to the dry ears of corn stored in the shed, or took rice out its sack to share with them. Every time I think about that old toothless woman and that old one-toothed man, my heart fills with joy.

My maternal grandparents teaching me to never think about color or race with hatred or contempt was an extraordinary gift.

I never knew for certain how much land my family owned until shortly after the Revolution, when I tried to understand the pains that came with the reforms and the redistributions of land. But I didn't understand. How could a young child understand why a government would want to take land away from the people who owned and cultivated it? How could I understand how much land three hundred five acres were?

THE MAGPIE AND THE FOX

Of course, Papá and Mamá had actual names, but no one in the family ever used them. None of their five daughters, their husbands, or their grandchildren.

They met when he was twelve and she was ten. They eloped *por la ventana*—Mamá escaping through the window in the middle of the night—just five years later, when he brought her to live at the farm amongst *los abuelitos* Elvira and Agustín, his three brothers, and his one peaceful sister with the musical voice, pure alabaster skin, waves of chocolate hair, and tourmaline eyes.

They were shrewd and ingenious. Their minds were quick and sharp. By 1950, four years before I was born, they had built an empire unlike anything else in that part of the countryside. Their home wasn't a four-room shack with waves of packed, tan clay on the floor, or a latrine to smell up the yard, as his brothers had. Instead, their new home was an enormous, long house that we all called *la finca*—the estate—with imported tile floors to welcome visitors, a refrigerator cooled by kerosene heat, a water tower, indoor plumbing, and even a modern shower, and a toilet that flushed.

They marked the extraordinary occasion by buying a shiny new red tractor and riding it to the nearby county courthouse to make their partnership legal. Afterward, they celebrated in the company of a crowd that stayed late into the night.

Papá was a fair man with a square forehead where his straight-across black hairline took hold. Though his temper was quick and hot, his anger never stayed long. He was a man able to diffuse and mediate, to appease and bestow. He was a generous man.

Maybe because of some remaining fear left behind from the illness after my birth, maybe because I was the only grandchild living away from the farm, maybe because I resembled him more than anyone else—I knew I was his favorite, just as Mother always knew that she was his favorite. One feels great power in believing that.

Alternating between a piercing stare and the smile in his eyes, he was a serious watchful owl that had also been granted the mischievous humor of a magpie.

He alone was able to tap behind the seriousness of my face and find the humor I always worked hard to hide—how he enjoyed teasing me time after time.

One afternoon, after returning home from the fields, he gave me a riddle to solve: "*¿A que vuelta se echa el perro?*" How many turns does a dog take before sitting down? And I thought, I can figure this out, it is only logic and math! In rapid repetition, I'd reply, "*¿Diez. cinco. catorce?*" He laughed, and Mamá laughed as she continued to stand by the stove. Finally, he looked at me and with a giggle said, "*A la última*"— after the last one.

I have never forgotten the afternoon he told me that riddle while sitting on the light-blue country kitchen chair he had made—*su taburete*—taking off the hard brown leather *polinas* protecting his legs to the knee, along with his boots, unlacing *las botas y las polinas,* all at the same time removing his dirt-filled socks and wiggling his toes. They were short, square, hairless toes. He had a name for each of those toes.

Mamá was quite a different animal altogether. Always busy, always moving, always laboring, like a beaver or a hedgehog, but with the nervous anxiety of a wild rabbit and the cunning quickness of a fox.

She was the businesswoman, the entrepreneur, the one who ran the small country store sandwiched between the kitchen and the rest of the house. The one who charged, customers and relatives alike, a nickel for the tray of ice cubes to cool the bucket of water they had just filled from the well by the kitchen's side door.

Many described her as *muy orgullosa*—an entitled and proud woman—but that is not how I think about her.

What I remember the most about her was her laughing while holding onto the stove's edge with her right hand to balance her exaggerated breasts, standing like a rare bird on its right foot, her knee locked in place, her left foot resting on the side of her right calf, brushing her stubborn coffee curls back while overtaking the room with her contagious laugh. *Mira que guanaja tú estás*—laughing like a silly turkey hen, people would say to her. To me, her laugh was as smooth going down as a warm fresh-baked buttered roll. Her laugh left me completely satisfied.

Still, she liked her great many rules, and easily bored, I enjoyed breaking them. In truth, I enjoyed ignoring all the rules. I always had a voracious ability for not acknowledging the stress and pain that I caused others with my constant refusals to conform—I would do anything not to conform, enjoying the power I held over everyone.

She wanted me to be a better listener, but listening always took too much time when all I was interested in was exploring what was just around the next turn. The present was just a moment away from being the past. But ahead—I always wanted to know what was just ahead. If I knew what was just ahead, then I could shape and predict what wasn't yet known, believing that by forecasting what was still to come, I'd have control over what was about to unfold. That if I had control, I'd be safe.

"Hijo, por qué nunca escuchas cuando te hablo?" Son, why don't you ever listen when I talk to you? Speaking in that unique way that she spoke, she'd repeat her mantra throughout my young life.

One summer, when I was ten but still quite small, knowing that there wasn't a thing that Papá would deny once I asked, I insisted that he saddle the pure-white and stubborn creature of a horse that Father had left behind so that I could ride him around the house. But that was a lie, for when no one was looking, defiantly and proudly, I took charge of my path to recreate the day that Father and I once had during a much happier time.

On that day when Papá saddled the horse for me, I left the perimeter of the house and spent hours visiting everyone I wanted to visit, uninvited and without their consent, ignoring the rolling eyes and comments from the relatives about how rebellious I was. *"Igualito a su madre...no escucha a nadie."* Just like his mother...does not listen to anyone. I told myself that I didn't care what they had to say—a lie that took me many years to confess.

Only now, as an adult looking back, can I finally understand how the independent and strong will that I had inherited from Mother would have been terrifying to Mamá. How my defiance made the rabbit inside her even more afraid.

Mother often lamented that her mother never loved her, but Mamá many times openly said that her daughter had been a difficult child to forgive and to love. Was I also difficult to forgive and to love?

THE ANDALUSIAN
AND THE CELT

I only met my paternal grandfather twice. His name was Juan, but everyone called him El Viejo Juan—Old Man Juan. He frightened me. I never opened my mouth to speak to him, so I know that I never called him anything. He spoke with the incomprehensible *Gallego* accent native to Northwest Spain, and every word out of his mouth sounded like a thunderous roar more that speech to me.

He was a tall man with the slicked-back short hair that Cubans like to call blond. His gray eyes stared piercingly at everyone from either side of his rigid beak-like nose. The top of his ears pointed out like those of a bat, and I was happy that I hadn't inherited such scary ears from him, even if I wished for his blond hair and light eyes. His face was ruddy and pink, from too much rum I supposed, as mother always complained.

By the time that I met him, my paternal grandparents had turned their modest farm over to their only other son, Nenico, and were living in the same small town—*el pueblecito*—where Mother and Father had married in the spring of 1952.

My first memory of El Viejo goes back to when I was six years old, during our visit to Abuela's house. Everyone always referred to it as her house, but I didn't know why at the time.

On that day of our visit, and while sitting at the evening table to eat, El Viejo got up and announced that he was going out and would not return that night. Father followed.

From the living room, I could hear angry sounds rather than words. These were followed by the *bang!* of the front door. Through it all, Abuela sat there and never spoke, but I remember looking at her face and feeling overwhelmed by the sadness in her eyes.

Years would pass before I learned about his routine— about him eating some of his evening meals with her before leaving to spend the night with his mistress and his other three younger sons at the house he rented for them across the street and five blocks away from Abuela's own house.

Father pointed her out to me on the street once. Her cinnamon—*canela*—skin glowed in the daylight. I thought she was beautiful. I never said anything to him about this, but to Mother I did.

To me, Abuela Dolores seemed like a saint. When she died, Mother said she had sent a message to tell me that she'd always be there to protect me and would always be there whenever I called her name.

Abuela and I never spoke about the things that were happening to me while she was alive, but without saying a word, I knew that she loved me and would have never asked anything in return. Even today, I feel her watching over me.

She was a *Morena* with high cheek bones a beautiful face and dark almond-shaped eyes that Father and I and Cousin Benita also shared. Waves of dark hair framed her face in the way that one day my hair would frame my face. She was a woman blessed with a *Flamenco* dignity in her stride.

A telegram arrived in the spring of 1965, right after I had just turned eleven years old, saying that she had asked for Mother and me to come, and we took the hours-long bus ride that same afternoon to be by her side.

When we arrived, we found her leaning over a hospital table by the side of her bed, and she was sweaty and wet, pale, and gray.

Timidly, I walked alone into her room and sat on her bed, not knowing what to do or what to say. Shaking, she slowly lifted her bony, wrinkled hand, as if needing all her strength to do so. After signaling me to come forward, she stroked my head before softly kissing my cheek. At Mother's insistence, we returned home the next day.

Two days later, when the news of her death came by telegram, I didn't cry. Instead, I cheered, and I sang. When Mother asked why, I said that I felt happy and not sad; she was at last free from her pain.

UNLOVED

Papá liked telling me that he named my mother Margarita because of the roundness of her face and because her eyes followed Mamá, just as a Daisy follows the light of sun. He used to tell me that she was always content when being held, but cranky whenever left alone in her crib. "*Es que a Margarita no la pueden dejar tranquila,*" he often joked. Still, and given that she responded to every touch, Mother was a baby who everyone wanted to hold. It is said that parents do not have a favorite child, but I always knew that Papá adored her and placed her before his other four girls.

Mother was two years old when her new sister was born. This had been a dangerously bloody delivery, and neither mother nor child were expected to survive.

As she'd openly recall during her dark days, Mother and her sister Cecilia shared the same crib, and she remembered reaching out to her mother, only to see her sister being picked up instead of her. Mother always ended this part of the story tearfully by describing the loneliness she felt.

When that painful moment had passed, she'd talk about her happy school days, and her expressive face lit up when describing her spinster teacher as being loving and kind. She ran a one-room schoolhouse where all the children from the nearby farms came together to learn.

As she portrayed herself, Mother seemed to me like a capricious and inquisitive child who lost interest and patience whenever the other children needed to hear the lesson multiple times. This, I understood well, for my own teachers were always telling me to be quiet and stop interrupting the class.

She often bragged about devouring every book and assignment given to her, and about her teacher advancing her to the next grade not once, but twice. It was then that her face lit up again with pride for having accomplished such a task.

Regrettably, perhaps because the family lived on a farm and far away from actual schools, cities, or cultural scenes, her school days ended when she reached the sixth grade at eight years of age.

Always at that point in her story, when recalling the end of her schooling, the clouds would return as Mother recalled how her life afterward, in a home filled with girls, became unbearable when Mamá decided she had to carry the greatest load. "*Yo no soy la criada.*" I'm not the maid, she always cried.

In such a mood, she spoke about how her older sister Consuelo was allowed to cry about this or that, or such as the work breaking her nails and harming her fair hands.

And of course, there was her crib mate, Cecilia, as she'd say, whom everyone thought as too fragile to lift the lightest of loads.

Mother usually paused at this point of the story, seemingly uncertain she wanted to go on complaining about her much younger sisters, Dulce and Nereida, who had arrived after another girl had been delivered stillborn. But this loss didn't seem to be as important to her as the remembrance of how her pampered sisters were never asked to contribute very much. Of course, none of this is how I remember any of them. In fact, Tia Dulce remains my most adored aunt.

For Margarita, my mother, the unjust pains of her childhood would grow into the mistrusts of her youth and the bitterness of her adulthood, and she took everyone along on her rides of exhausting euphoria and devastating lows. As difficult as she was, I know that she alone wasn't at fault. She was also driven there by my father's own inability to cope.

An Accusation

At nearly fourteen, Mother was no more than a bony girl with unnoticeable breasts, long gangly arms, skinny ankles, and wispy short bangs across her forehead—she looked like a boy more than a girl. Given that Papá liked keeping her by his side as he performed his chores around the farm, people gossiped about her being his only son, and this was always very upsetting for her.

By then, the effervescence of her soul, so obvious during her years in school amongst all her friends, had been replaced by angry outbursts which brought her into constant conflicts with Mamá, who insisted on a home built upon routine, obedience, and work.

In contrast, sixteen-year-old Consuelo had bloomed into the affable beauty that everyone wanted to love. I, too, thought she was beautiful, even if I was never able to feel any close affection from her. I remember saying once that, in her wedding picture, she looked like Hedy Lamarr.

Word of her beauty had gotten around, and many potential suitors began showing up at the house. Every time, Papá rejected them, believing she was too young to marry or date. That is, until Reinaldo appeared on the scene. He was the son of a prosperous landowner who lived near the sugar mill at least a half-hour ride on horseback.

Because of such an important connection, this black-haired boy with eyes as clear as the morning sky was allowed to visit Consuelo if they stayed on opposite sides of the living room's Dutch door, and if they never held hands or touched.

Fascinated with this beautiful boy, Mother took to lingering around every time Reinaldo visited the house. Being friendly and polite, he acknowledged her, though Consuelo refused to acknowledge or even look at her. Her sister had learned that this was the best plan, for if you gave Margarita any attention, she'd become annoyingly clingy and never leave a person's side. *"Si le das un dedo se te coje la mano"*—if you give her one finger, she will take the full hand, Consuelo cried. This rejection only made things worse as Mother strengthened her resolve. She could not help it, feeling as if Reinaldo had secretly poisoned her with a drug.

No witnesses or chaperones were there, and no one knew where Mother had gone until she returned home in an agitated state. Her dress was partly torn over the left breast and covered in dirt. *"Mira, ¡que Reinaldo me atacó!"* Look, Reinaldo attacked me! she told everyone.

Each sister took sides at once. Consuelo reached for Mamá, and Mother clung to Papá while the three younger girls giggled and did all they could to hide.

"Ya sabes cómo es ella. Siempre mintiendo y siempre inventando las cosas para que le den lo que quiere. ¡Di la verdad! ¿Qué hiciste? ¿Por qué tú dices eso?" Consuelo said, accusing her sister of lying to get whatever she wanted, as she had done all her life.

Papá sent away for a doctor to examine Mother, and despite him not finding anything wrong with her, she'd not stop her cries and laments. The authorities were then called.

Everyone was present at the inquest as Reinaldo was questioned and denied all the charges that Mother had made. In the end, given that she was so young and that nothing else could really be done, he was sentenced to jail time and taken away.

But Mother had brought a great shame to the family and to each of the girls. And so, she too was sent away to live with *los abuelitos* in a secluded corner of the great farm, and away from her sisters, cousins, visitors, and friends.

From that day forward, she blamed Mamá, but never Papá for sending her away, never believing that her father was responsible for her pain.

RECONCILIATION

M other had been away for a year when diphtheria visited
her. Patiently, death stood by her bedside, hoping each
breath she took was to be her last one.

She was too ill to be move, and Consuelo, who had
refused to visit her all that time, begged to be sent to los
abuelito's house to care for her. Papá had been the only one
in the family to visit Mother, but given her grave condition,
her sister, engulfed by anxiety and remorse over her earlier
actions, desperately wanted a chance to make amends before
her sister could die.

For several days, Mother could not speak, and with every
painful breath that she took, Consuelo, and not Mamá, stayed
there with her until eventually death stopped his pursuit, and
the smell from its foul breath disappeared from the house.

One day, when Mother became coherent at last, the
sisters spoke, but not about the sins from the past.

UNFORGIVEN

Another year would pass before Mother was allowed to return home, and few knew who she was, for she had become a handsome young woman with voluptuous breasts. Gifted with a humorous and intoxicating charm, her three younger sisters hung onto her every word and mimicked her every action.

This new sisterly adoration became a great concern for Mamá as she worried that her daughter's shame had remained unresolved. She understood, perhaps more than anyone else, how important it was for Mother to marry as soon as a man who wanted her could be found.

Still, no man asked, and Mamá feared not just for Mother, but for the reputation and the future of the rest of her girls. "*Donde hay una hay muchas.*" Where there is one, there are many, the superstitious country people liked to say.

CANON

My father, Julian, was the second boy in a family of five children that included just one surviving younger boy. He was only four years old when his oldest brother, Carlos, died, and Father dealt with this loss by becoming very protective of his younger brother, who was born two years later. This protecting drive extended to his mother because El Viejo was an abusive man who liked to shout orders and demand perfection, while always insisting that he had never been properly obeyed.

To this day, I think of my uncle Nenico as the most beautiful man I ever saw. He was svelte and had a face full of angles, highlights, and shades. His eyes were a vivid shade of blue, and his head overflowed with gentle black waves. He was cheerful, easygoing, and charmed everyone with his playful laugh.

In contrast, Father was always serious. His intelligence was unusual and not obvious to everyone. He was socially awkward and easily hurt. He understood things in rigid, absolute terms, and life's gray mysteries didn't live comfortably in his mind.

He was also loyal and ever-present for his male friends, and the quiet friendships he developed in his childhood would remain with him into adulthood. Even so, he had no difficulties cutting off a friend if he believed that he had been injured in some form.

Shy and awkward around girls, he trusted his beauty would mask the inadequacies he felt, never aware that his overly expressive eyes betrayed him every time.

He had great difficulty reading, writing, and recalling the lessons in class, and these limitations made him impatient with the world, always leaving him feeling frustrated and chastised.

One day, when he felt his teacher had embarrassed him beyond what he could take, he walked out of the schoolhouse and never returned to complete the fifth grade. Instead, he returned to work at his family's farm, where he was happy to hide, never wishing for more than what he had already received from life. All he wanted to do was marry, build a house, and spend his existence within his own plot of land.

Father was a laborer, an assembly line worker, content with the orthodoxy of his life.

INTOXICATION

Small dances—*los bailecitos*—took place at any number of places. Some in private homes by pushing the furniture to the walls. Others in what foreigners may think of as a barn, where it was a tradition for the young women to carry a *taburete* on their head, so as to make sure they didn't have to stand. These forever jubilant girls marched together to the dance, wearing their best dresses and balancing the upside-down chairs on their head, all while trying not to crush the flowers or broaches in their hair or their strategically placed curls.

The big *bailes*—the large dances that took place at the local sugar mill's assembly hall—normally came around twice a year, and they brought young people from many parts of the county or the province at large. Most often, they took place during Christmas and at the end of Holy Week—*Semana Santa*. Musicians traveled from location to location to entertain the large crowds. At these dances, lemonade, sodas, and alcohol flowed and the music constantly played.

At these formal dances, girls and boys stood separately while chaperons looked on with critical eyes, ready to protect a girl's reputation and good name, ready to restrain any girl who strayed away from the rigid guidelines. No loud conversations or bouncing about were allowed in any form. The chaperons took careful measures to ensure that the girls were not the center of the crowd's attention, ridicule, or scorn.

Mother had worked nonstop on her debut dress, taking full advantage of the correspondence dressmaker course that she had completed while in exile at *los abuelitos*. She was delighted with the results—a long gown made of sheer white organza over fine linen, its top gathered into delicate folds that enhanced her full breasts. The rounded shoulder line was decorated with a garland of eyelet through which she had laced delicate ribbons in pale mint and rose. The dress accentuated her small waist via a royal blue satin sash that flowed down the side of her skirt.

On the day of the dance, she arranged her hair high, pinning it on the sides, but allowing the back to flow down to just above her shoulders because this style best showed off the embroidered silk Juliette bonnet that crowned her head. A gold evening watch on her left wrist, and round wire-rim glasses that were all the rage, completed the look. She even secretly applied some of the perfume that Consuelo had been given as a birthday gift. This was fine, she told herself, because Consuelo wasn't going to the dance. How would she know? Standing in front of Mamá's three-mirror vanity, Mother was sure that she'd be the belle of the ball.

Father had also fussed as he prepared for the dance, fully aware of how handsome he looked in his four-pocket linen *guayabera* shirt that Abuela had starched and pressed until it could easily stand on its own. He also wore linen trousers with two-tone black and white shoes, and slicked his black hair with plenty of brilliantine. He wore no aftershave or cologne because real men never wore any such nonsense.

The mill's hall was a long rectangular room with cement floors, a door on every wall, and tall windows all around. Chairs and benches were lined up against the walls. When Mother entered the room, she felt every gaze focus on her.

And indeed, she became the center of attention, thanks to her beautiful dress, her looks, and a manic energy that made her stand out from every other girl at the dance.

From his corner of the room, and amongst his friends, Father's gaze followed the exuberant eighteen-year-old as she danced, flirted, and teased her way through the hall. He watched as many boys gathered around her to ask her for a dance, and then watched the crowd as a feeding frenzy took hold until the chaperons put a stop to her flight.

Overpowered by the rush of blood that made his thighs tremble, Father was as if in a trace. Until that moment, he believed that his aloofness had served him well at social gatherings. But this time, he felt an overwhelming desire to act. Finding courage in a strong drink, he asked Mother to the floor, even though he had never really learned how to dance. In truth, he could dance well enough, but being watched by the crowd was terrifying to him. He was sure that everyone would see his awkwardness and laugh. His fears were not unfounded, because as soon as the song was over, Mother laughed before leaving his side. But had she laughed at him, or simply laughed nervously to hide the rush of electricity she felt? This question was to linger unanswered in the air, as no other words were exchanged between them that day.

During the journey home, all Mother could think about was the attention the boys had showered on her. She had forgotten about dancing with Father—he was only one of the many boys she had danced with that night.

She was too deep in her own thoughts to be aware that no one spoke during the journey back to the farm. She didn't see the embarrassment on the face of her cousins, her uncle, or her one maternal aunt who had taken her to the dance.

"*¡No más bailes o fiestas para usted!*" Papá said in a formal voice, the moment he heard how Mother had behaved. There were to be no more dances or parties for her.

Mother didn't understand, but told herself that her father's temper would pass, and that she be triumphant in the end—she was used to getting her way with him.

Mother was wrong. This time, he could not possibly change his mind and allow her example to corrupt his other girls. Mother could not see how selfish she had been.

Opportunity

I t had been two weeks since the dance, and Mother's three younger sisters sheepishly kept trying to find a moment to be alone with her. They were dying to hear how it had gone at the dance and why Papá had acted so angrily. In fact, Mamá was angrier—she wasn't speaking to her. However, in such a tense atmosphere, her sisters knew better than to be caught asking questions or offering their sister any support. As for her older sister Consuelo, she took Mamá's side, as always, and kept away from everyone.

Mother stood alone in the house, feeling as sad as when she had been sent away. As then, she could not understand the punishment that had been inflicted on her.

It was a tradition that when a young man found himself interested in an unmarried girl, he was expected to write a letter to her parents asking for permission to court, and this is what Father did. His best friend Ramón arrived on horseback with letter in hand.

Consuelo, sitting on the front porch, sifting all the little pebbles out of the rice before rinsing and cooking it for the evening meal, noticed the broad-shouldered blond, but no words were exchanged between then because Mamá, standing behind the kitchen's Dutch door, had also noticed him and instantly called her daughter into the house.

The letter remained unopened until that afternoon, after Papá returned home from his daily chores. They didn't read it until he had washed up and changed his clothes, for that was the time when he and Mamá always sat alone to discuss the events of the day or go over the books. None of the girls knew who Ramón was, or who the letter was from.

Papá and Mamá read the letter, but didn't share the information with Mother or the girls. They had no idea who Father was, and thought it best not to say anything until the necessary inquiries had been made. Who were his parents? What was his bloodline? What was known about his family's farm? How much land did they own? Was there enough land for him to support his own family and a wife? These were all delicate questions, and it took some time to find the proper spies and for them to return with the facts. They recognized the handwriting from other letters in the past, given that it had been penned by the one professional scribe whose services were used by everyone. Almost everyone, that is, for Papá and Mamá knew how to read and write. Still, they didn't hold this fact against Father because he had paid for the letter to be composed, which spoke about the seriousness of his intent.

Responses came back a week later, and while it was agreed that Father's family wasn't as affluent as Mother's own—poor, even, in the eyes of many—this was too good of a chance to miss. Father's character would become clear soon enough once they got to meet him and get to know him better. It was only then that Mother saw the letter for the first time.

Running out into the yard and away from her sisters to be alone, she skipped through all the wordy formalities to the part where Father introduced himself. She only cared that someone had asked for permission to start counting her.

"...*Yo soy el hijo mayor del señor Don Juan Cruz y Álvares de la finca San Cristóbal. Quiero pedirle su permiso para visitar a su hija Margarita...*"

Mother felt flattered, ignoring the reality that she only had a vague memory of who Father was. It didn't matter. What better way to prove to everyone that her behavior at the dance hadn't been inappropriate at all?

COURTSHIP

Father arrived at the farm in a cream linen suit, a yellow and maroon tie, two-tone black and white shoes, and a Panama hat in his hand. His hair was neatly packed down with brilliantine, and his face was closely shaved except for a perfectly shaped thin mustache. He was a sensual being able to arouse those around him, regardless of what gender they were. All he had to do was turn his head down and cock it to one side before looking up with longing in his eyes—that was his charm.

Invited to come into the formal part of the newly built house displaying comforts that he had never seen, Father spoke to Mamá in the traditionally expected small talk.

"¡Qué calor tenemos!" and "¿Y su familia está bien?" he asked, limiting the conversation to the hot weather, and inquiring after her family, always taking care to use the formal *Su* when addressing her, instead of the familiar *Tu*.

Then Papá spoke, and more small talk followed about Father's family and their farm, and about visiting hours and days. Father didn't know that the decision to allow him to date their daughter had already been made by them.

Through it all, Mother and her sisters listened from behind a nearby wall.

This was an important moment for the family. Even more important for Mother, as she was the first—not her oldest sister, Consuelo—to have a boy officially come to the house. Mother believed she had become the center of the home.

With formalities over and permissions out of the way, Mother was brought out and told to sit with Father for a time while Mamá sat within eyesight—an awkward moment for two people who were no more than strangers to each other at the time.

Mother recognized Father at once, remembering his awkward movements on the dance floor, but also how his touch had made her feel. This memory made her look forward to his visits, even if they had to take place with Mamá sitting just on the other side of the great hall.

It didn't take long for her to be disappointed by his quiet demeanor and the seriousness of his face. In silence, she wondered if he was the person that she could be happy with. But it was too late to change her mind because Father and Papá had quickly built a bond that seemed to others like that of a father and son. How could she walk away from this situation without admitting defeat and angering everyone?

MANIPULATION

More than a year had passed when Father arrived at the farm with a bundle of clothes under his arm—*con un bulto de ropa*. It was lunchtime, and Papá was in the house. He stepped outside, and the two men spoke for a long time before Father came into the kitchen and sat at the table to eat the lunch plate that Mamá—as if knowing that company was coming—had prepared for him.

Father explained that El Viejo had been keeping a mistress in the nearest town, and of how a confrontation between then had taken place that day. He then went on, after griding his teeth in anger for a moment, to explain how the old man had chased him out of the house with a machete in hand, all the time screaming that he was never to return. Father said he needed a place to live, and begged Papá and Mamá to let him stay and work for them at the farm. They agreed.

The kitchen and provision rooms were separated from the main part of the house by a large door that bolted from inside. With no danger of Father sneaking in to visit Mother during the night, he was told he could sleep on a folding cot they could set up for him.

Rumors of scandals began to circulate as soon as Father had moved into the house, and without delay, a wedding was planned. The speculations remained for two years, until I was born.

ORDINARY

My parent's simple marriage ceremony took place in the nearest town to the farm—the same town where Abuela, El Viejo, and his mistress would one day live. The affair had to be a modest one, so as to not stir up gossip concerning Mother having been sent away. That was a secret that needed to be kept at all costs. Only a quiet family meal waited for them upon their return to the farm.

What no one ever guessed was that Father knew about the wild girl and how her accusations had put Reinaldo in jail. In fact, both men had grown up on adjacent farms. However, he didn't learn about her identity until the day after the dance.

This didn't matter to him because he wasn't only marrying the girl who made his thighs tremble, but he was gaining a new father and family at the same time. Being a poor farmer, entering an affluent family would be a great achievement for him.

Besides, he had confided in Papá and was sure that, between her parents' commitment and his, Margarita could be easily controlled. After all, the plan was for them to always live at the farm. As a married woman, busy with childbirth and raising children, she'd never find an opportunity to misbehave.

Mother had made her wedding dress, and together with Consuelo and Mamá, they sat on the flat bed that Papá had hitched to the back of the tractor. People could sit on it quite easily when at its lowest position before he raised it up and drove off. This way, the riders sat above the dust, stones, or twigs along the road.

That *pueblecito* where the wedding took place wasn't even an actual town. Rather, it was a group of houses and storefronts along a single main street, with just two or three streets on either side. These streets disappeared within a couple blocks, into vast tracks of flat land. Its Main street ran for about a mile between the cross county two-lane highway to the railroad tracks.

The justice of the peace's office was in the front of a small house on the main street. In attendance were Mother, Consuelo, Father, his brother Nenico, and Father's best friend, Ramón who began courting Consuelo shorty after Father had been welcomed into the home.

Once the brief ceremony was over, the party walked to the photography shop just a few paces away for the couple to have their picture taken, ordering several copies for their families and friends. A larger portrait was also ordered, along with a mother-of-pearl frame for it to be prominently displayed in the living room of their eventual home.

The next morning, Father returned to his work at the farm and Mother returned to a life that seemed as unchanged as the day before she had wed.

But this wasn't completely true, for the kitchen's back storeroom where Father slept had been painted a cheerful shade of green. A double-sized bed and a small chest, two chairs, a side table, and a washstand had also been placed there for them.

Mother had embroidered a new set of pale-yellow sheets and matching pillowcases with a beautiful floral pattern, and the bed looked beautiful every time it was made. As a small child, I used to trace their pattern of white daisies and blue violets with my finger.

Father was visibly happy, and Mother seemed content. Her new status as a married woman had granted her added importance. She even saw herself to be on equal footing with Mamá.

Theirs was a content and quiet life with days consumed by chores, cleaning, and cooking, and evenings filled with long conversations around the kitchen table by the light of the kerosene lamps.

Despite it all, when alone in their own room, my mother, Margarita, and my father, Julian, had created an untroubled home for themselves.

DANGER

After more than a year of trying to conceive, Mother's pregnancy became a source of boundless joy, but she also bled on and off and was plagued by all sorts of undefinable pains.

Given the stress of her situation, everyone lived in dread, convinced that her unborn child would not survive to full term. Consuelo, who had married Ramón six months after my parents' wedding in an elaborate celebration feast, had lost her first child, a girl, during the sixth month of her pregnancy, and Mamá's own history of stillbirths lingered unspoken in everyone's thoughts.

Mother had been just old enough to watch the full crisis and experience the loss of her last sister to die at birth, and such young memories of imagined rivers of blood flowing from her mother had become a recurring nightmare for her.

Early into her seventh month, the local country doctor said that she needed to stay at the provincial capital's hospital maternity ward and be closely watched until I was born. This was a needed but scary proposition. What if something went wrong during their ride there?

Mother had lived her life without traveling more than a few miles from the farm, and had no idea what waited there for her—the north shore city by the beautiful bay was an unknown and distant planet to her.

After dropping Mother off at the hospital, Father quickly returned to the farm, feeling great relief in knowing that Mother was at last safe and in well-trained hands.

After being on her own for a time, Mother began to remember how she felt after being sent away by Mamá. Feeling abandoned once again, all she could do that rainy evening was stay in bed and cry.

The next morning, she found the courage to pull back the curtains and step out into the ward.

CONFINEMENT

A long hallway ran down the center of the maternity ward. Creamy butter-colored iron beds were flanked by a procession of tall windows along the outer walls that brought in the sunlight. An envelope of glossy laurel-green paint reached up to waist level, and then the same buttery yellow of the beds reached up to the ceiling. Large fans, all in a row, performed their quiet duty in rhythmic accord. Starched, kind nurses and severely veiled nuns ran the show. Doctors in white tops performed their dignified roles. Robed Catholic priests walked about, busily attending to their required daily calls. Yet not everyone prayed and not everyone communed. Some of the women prayed on silent alters to gods officially condemned by the church.

The women's needs were anticipated and met, their days intended to be comprised entirely of untroubled moments of calm—and for those in possession of a soul at rest, it was so. For others, this was a much more challenging task.

There were no private rooms in this maternity ward. Expectant mothers lived as just one amongst many more. That was the golden rule of this hospital. It was what the European-blooded white women were told, and what the mixed-race women were told, and what the women whose ethnicity wasn't clearly known were told. It was what the black women were told. No fights or arguments were allowed. Everyone was equally expected to behave and conform.

But expectations and reality rarely lived in harmony— especially in a community of women with nothing to occupy their days except their own thoughts, worries, and insecurities.

This stress made the restless women loud, and they often got into brawls when their class and skin differences were pointed out, and then they wounded one another with the cruelty of their words. This pecking order was arranged and rearranged with every new expectant mother who arrived, until there was little chance for any woman to rest.

Discovery

amá told all her girls that the distance to the hospital was too great for any unmarried young woman to travel there alone. As for Papá, with the need to keep up with his many chores, he could not find the time to take the girls there himself. Even Father visited only once during those weeks of forced separation and rest. All alone, Mother found herself lacking the skills to fight the quarreling. Nevertheless, she soon discovered a talent for charming the priests, the doctors, the nuns, the nurses, and even some of the patients.

Mother saw them as an audience waiting for her to perform, just like the audience she had found during her brief days in school. Then, as she began to talk about the pools of blood on her mother's bed, she saw how everyone felt sorry for her.

She was no longer afraid. Instead, she embraced the excitement of being away at a place that was different, and she began to dream about an unknown life in a distant city away from the farm. It was in this moment that her newborn fantasies begged to live on, surrounded by all the attention they deserved. However, a kick, a squirm, or a movement inside her belly would inventively remind her of my imminent birth. My movements filled her heart with sadness because she didn't see a way to nurture her dreams.

But these dreams continued to cry out, as all hungry newborns cry for their mother's breast. And so Mother promised to feed them in secret, vowing to free them one day, not understanding the journey that such a promise would force her and the family to take.

CONTENTMENT

The miracle from the light flooding the kitchen had passed, and everything was silent at the house. Mother sewed, Father sat by the radio at the end of his day, and Tía Cecilia brewed her strong afternoon coffee while I continued to draw.

My third birthday that February came without a celebration, but the arrival of *las tías* from the farm on that same day felt like a gift to me. Tía Nereida left the next morning with Mother in tow, but Tía Dulce stayed behind. Everything changed overnight.

My memories of what followed are brief, but clear flashes in time as I remember being held, being fed, feeling safe, singing songs, and clapping my hands to a rhyme whose words I can no longer recall.

Tía Dulce was the first adult to ever take me to play on the swings, the slides, and the enormous sandbox at the one corner of the nearby park. I felt great happiness being with her at the park.

Those days when Mother was away were the peaceful days when Father sat at the edge of my bed. Without speaking while rubbing my back, slowly, gently, and with kindness and heart, he stayed with me until sleep easily came.

But Mother eventually returned from the farm with Papá at her side, and those happy days were replaced with slow, solemn days after Tía Dulce stepped back and allowed Mother to return to her role. Mother was cold and detached; she was like a stranger to me.

They were also the days when Papá stayed with us for a time, and I felt boundless joy whenever he sat me on his lap and bounced me up and down on his knee, laughing with me.

BLISS

Things changed very quickly after Papá arrived. It wasn't yet Cuban spring when we moved into our new apartment, just six blocks away and a few houses down from Benita's. I remember the move. I remember Mother being happy. I remember her smiles. I felt what she felt.

Our new home was at the end of an alley that wasn't narrow but wide. In this alley, there was no hard cement under my feet, but deep maroon tiles crossed with gold ribbons holding green curvy vines with leaves. Ours was the only apartment right behind an elegant hunter-green house facing the block.

So much was different. Our joint living and dining rooms were large and bright. There were three bedrooms, a bathroom, a kitchen, a back patio enclosed by a tall wall. By the living room window at the front of the house there was an enormous Admiral television cabinet with the smallest of screens and a rabbit ears antenna for Father to constantly adjust.

I loved having my own room with my own window at the front of the house. I loved having my own big-boy bed. I loved having my own *escaparate* with its many drawers and a rod to hang my clean clothes on, so big that I could step in, close the door, and disappear inside. I loved my own baby-chick yellow headboard that Papá built for me and brought back from the farm. I loved its built-in side drawers and its built-in shelves behind the pillows where I rested my head noon and night. These were the shelves I quickly filled with the storybooks that Tía Dulce had bought for me, the pretty books she had enjoyed reading to me, the captivating books with all the colors and pictures and faces always happy and bright.

SAFETY

Our new apartment and my new headboard may have been Papá's next gifts to me, but the money he left behind was also his gift because it allowed Mother to stay home and fill her days just caring for me.

And his money would continue to come, but only if Mother and Father found a way to stop fighting and fill their home with love. It would only continue to come if Mother and Father focused on me and not on their throbbing dark thoughts.

Every morning, I waited until Cousin Sandra arrived. She stayed with me while Mother prepared breakfast for us. There were runny, soft-boiled eggs standing upright in their own rounded mustard-yellow plastic cups, toasted store-bought bread slices heaping with cream cheese, and hot chocolate milk to dip our toast in.

Then, with breakfast completed, the dishes were quickly replaced with coloring pencils and books for Sandra and me to practice our art.

At mid-morning, we walked down the block to visit Benita, drop Sandra off, and happily receive her kisses and hugs. Our visit completed, Mother and I brought Father lunch at his produce stand.

Afterward, we visited the park for me to play on the slides and swing on the green-bottomed seat where I flew high in the air, not feeling frightened at all.

Once playtime was over, we returned home for my lunch and a nap to be followed by an afternoon bath and a crisp set of clothes.

After dressing up, we strolled past the pretty houses on the block so Mother could show me off to the well-attired neighbors at every stop. I'd soak in their praises about my looks and my poise.

Once home, I watched Mother cook as she waited for Father to arrive from work, followed by relaxing meals at my pedestal table, surrounded by a family that seemed happy and talked.

Then the pampering would start by Mother cutting my steak and my chicken into tiny morsels that were easy to chew. For dessert, she popped the seeds from juicy red grapes sitting inside a sparkling blue metal bowl. I sat there as a young bird sits on its nest, waiting to be fed one grape at a time.

Once the meal was over, Father would sit in his chair and watch the ballgame on the new television set. I was so happily sitting right next to him on my child-sized silver frame chair upholstered in gold. Clinging to Father's thigh, I held the stuffed giraffe that Papá had given me on the day he arrived with Mother from the farm.

At bedtime, Mother dressed me in fresh pajamas, and I jumped into bed to listen to her bedtime stories until the slumbering cherubs tugged me to sleep.

I was so happy that I often awoke in the middle of the night to stand at the window to commune with the moon and follow its path.

BIGOTRY

Father, I noticed, seemed so happy from behind the counter of his produce stand, enjoying the procession of patrons in a culture where shopping was done every day because the idea of a supermarket had apparently never occurred to anyone. Grandmothers and maids, mothers and daughters—they all came with their lists in hand.

On Wednesdays, Father would set aside potatoes and chunks of pumpkin for Doña Alfonsa because that was the day when she made her delicious red bean soup.

On Fridays, Señora Luisa counted on him for the ripest plantains for her famous maduros treat. I loved eating her fried plantains because they were never overcooked or bitter, as Mother's tended to be.

Men also stopped, not to shop, but to discuss the events of the day, and within the small world he had made, Father felt as content and safe as during his working days at the farm.

Standing behind the tall counter with a smile on his face, I can clearly remember the day when he cut a gigantic watermelon slice for me. I also remember how quickly Mother snatched it from my hands, afraid that the juice would stain my heavily starched white cotton shirt. Father never worried about staining his shirt because laundry was a woman's work. Doing the laundry and keeping the house clean was her job, not mine or his, Father liked to say.

Even so, no matter how much I looked forward to visiting him, these times came with an entry price because he expected me to remain quiet and repress my inquisitive drive before paying attention to me.

Then, only when I was quiet and still, Father would be loving to me. Only then, Father would teach me and speak to me about things. Only then did Father talk to me about the things that he hated and the things he believed. His most pressing lessons were from the old tales, the old fears, and the old prejudices about someone of questionable race passing as white.

My confusion was evident the first time he took my right index finger and rubbed it on the top of my left hand, his eyes widening. That was the sign, he explained—the way to silently tell others that someone was passing for white. Throughout his entire life, he insisted this was an important lesson to learn.

SHAME

I may have been only three in the summer of 1957, but I knew what school was, and I knew where it was. Every day, on the way to visit Father, or on our walks to the park, Mother and I passed the two-story house painted in bright yellow. I even met my future kindergarten teacher Raquel once, during one of our walks.

Me attending a private school was especially important for Mother because it signaled our ascendance into the middle class. Never mind that Father ran a produce stand, or that we were from a farm. Even at such an early age, I somehow understood that it was important for me to fit in and succeed.

Mother spent the summer making my new school uniform, a pair of tan-colored short pants, a white shirt with the school patch on its left arm, and a tomato-red scarf.

After the pediatrician insisted that I wear orthopedic shoes, Mother took me to the famous specialty store in old Havana to be measured, and ordered a new pair of expensive boots. Not until we went back for a final fitting did I realize how ugly they were—all black, round at the front, and hot. I wore a version of those torturous things until I turned twelve, and refused to ever wear them again.

The Sunday before school was to start had been an untroubled day. Mother, who had made *arroz con pollo* and flan, along with Father and Tía Cecilia, were happy to welcome Benita, Celestino, Sandra, and her parents into the house and to celebrate our important day.

After the meal, Father, Celestino, and Sandra's father sat on the alleyway to talk, while the women chatted inside the house and Sandra and I sat at our special table to draw and dream about us starting school the very next day.

When Mother and I arrived at the school, the sidewalk and the porch were overflowing with parents and children, but they were all strangers to me. From out of nowhere, a woman that I had never seen grabbed my hand and started to take me away. She was a large woman with a powdered, cratered face, and her hair was like a helmet of tight black curls.

I looked at her, looked at Mother, held tightly with my free hand onto the porch railing, and began to cry, "*¡No tú! ¡Quiero mi Papi! ¿Donde esta Papi?*" Again and again, calling for Father to come.

Father's stand was less than a block away, and so they sent for him. Before I knew it, he was kneeling beside me. Calmly, he pried my fingers from the fence. Then, taking a hold of my hand, he walked me to my new classroom to let me sit next to Cousin Sandra, who was already there waiting for me. As he left, we both smiled at him and waved him goodbye. I felt safe.

That afternoon, when Mother and I walked past the school, I saw workmen removing the porch railings and gate. When I returned to school the next day, they were gone and everyone was staring at me.

I knew then that all my kicking and screaming the previous day had forced the school to make this radical change, proving to them that I was no more than an uneducated peasant's son that didn't know how to behave.

KINDNESS

Raquel, my kindergarten teacher, was the first person outside the family to be affectionate with me. Her actions showed me that the world outside my confusing home could be pleasant and calm. A peaceful, happy place, her classroom was full of joyful music—a sanctuary of songs we sang gleefully as she played the piano for us.

Each morning, we gathered around the piano to learn a new song. Later, she'd read aloud to us, pausing at the end of each page to show us the illustration as she pointed at the text.

Often, in the afternoon, we took out our crayons and coloring books or large sheets of white paper on which we freely expressed ourselves by drawing whatever vision was running through our minds.

When the holidays rolled around, we decorated a tree with garlands of brightly colored paper chains that we constructed together as part of a team.

Open-hearted Raquel was always happy. So whenever I felt unsure or unsafe, I reached for her hand. I relished her kind touch and the soothing gentleness of her voice.

DESPAIR

As soon as I started school, arguments between Mother and Father flared up, becoming one more daily task on their list to cross off before bedtime. Each day, she lashed out, shouting the same hurtful insults at Father in her attempt to win every argument.

Having so much free time on her hands while I was in school left her confused about her role in the house. Unable to confront her own demons, she found it easier to blame others for the uncontrollable rage she felt.

Father tuned her out when he was home and stayed away as much as he could, never sharing his feelings with her. Unable to escape, I was left to soak up her frantic energy.

Sundays were everyone's only day off, and both Tía Cecilia and Father were always ready with their plans. However, Mother was seldom included in these because she was expected to stay home and care for me.

Early on Sunday mornings, Tía Cecilia left the house to spend her day doing things in town with her friends from the sewing factory—a place where she'd end up working her entire life.

Ready to be anywhere but in the house, Father spent his Sundays at Benita's, playing dominoes with the guys. They played for hours while Benita cooked and refilled coffee cups, happy to entertain the men, their children, and wives. Mother would never attend, believing that by staying at home, she was making everyone feel the rejection she felt. "*Yo no soy una viuda,*" she'd say, telling everyone that she wasn't a widow but a wife.

On the few Sundays she went to Benita's, Mother complained about her life to the women there, who openly raised their brows and rolled their eyes in that unique gesture that Cuban women use—a combination of wisdom, judgment, and pride. Loyal and steady, Benita insisted the women stop. Quickly, they obeyed, respectful of her fidelity.

Occasionally, Father went to the nearby movie theater after spending his morning playing dominos. Mother always begged to go, but he refused to take us with him because I often cried, claiming that the racket was disgraceful and difficult for him to face. Instead, Mother remained behind with nothing to do but house chores and caring for me. She'd pass the time by and singing along with the emotional Bolero songs playing on the radio, but her singing wasn't pleasant or soothing. Even though she was a melodic alto, she sang in the fast, high-pitch manner that she had always used when singing her favorite *guajiro* songs at the farm. From morning until the time Father came home, she obsessively sang *Bésame Mucho*, as if this fear-filled song about being left behind by a lover brought some comfort to her.

Frustrated, she spent hours over the stove, cooking giant pots of chicken and yellow rice that she decorated with canned tender young peas and red pimento strips.

When Father returned from the theater feeling recharged, she'd use his demeanor as one more reason to fight. Once a fight was over, Father happily returned to the rituals he followed every day: a shower, putting on pajama bottom pants, a sleeveless underwear top, slippers, eating dinner in silence, sitting alone by the television to watch the baseball game or the boxing match broadcast as loudly as one of their fights.

JOY

I distinctly remember the morning of January 6, 1958, just before I was to turn four years old. For days, if not months, I had been warned to be good since the three wise men—*los magos*—were keeping a close eye on everything I did and said. I didn't have a clear picture of who they were. However, I was told that they dressed in fine golden robes and wore jeweled turbans and crowns on their heads. The tales went on with Father saying that they'd arrive riding their two camels and one shinny white horse. All that spectacle and fanfare certainly mattered, but what I cared about the most was trusting that they'd leave behind an endless number of toys. I tried to force myself to stay awake the night before so I could see them come in, but sleep overcame my resolve.

Rising early before the sun broke through my bedroom window, I jumped out of bed and walked through the shadows to the door's threshold. Rubbing the sleep from my eyes until they had fully adjusted to the dark, I was thrilled to discover the mountain of toys waiting for me. And with all the furniture pushed aside, *los magos* had created a path for me to walk through the wonders there in front of me— my reward for being good, though I didn't exactly know what being good was.

Nothing was wrapped. Instead, each toy was placed on top of its box, making it easy for my gaze to bounce from one toy to the next until I saw the bright-red concrete mixer. I rushed to it. Back and forth, I rolled it on the floor to make the drum spin. But when I noticed the cowboy set laid out on a chair waiting for me, I dropped the mixer immediately. I liked cowboy things because watching those shows on TV was one of the few things that Father and I ever did together as father and son.

Without delay, I tied the orange bandanna around my neck, fastened the thick-buckled belt that held a gun at each side, and pulled the fringed gloves on. With my white cowboy hat perched atop my head, I was one of the good guys.

Busy in my happy thoughts, I didn't notice Mother, Father, and Tía Cecilia entering the room until I turned around and saw them standing right next to me, just as the sun cut through the open blinds, spotlighting the joyful tears running down Mother's face.

I was content. I was satisfied. In that quiet moment, I didn't want or need anything else in my life.

Dread

The house was never at rest during the brief weeks between the magi's Epiphany visit and the day when my fourth birthday came. I loved all the commotion because I knew that the preparations were all about me. After hearing that Tía Dulce, and even Tía Nereida, had sent word that they were planning to come, I was thrilled, and when Tía Consuelo and Tío Ramón walked in the day before with two-year old cousin Nicolás, I could not believe my good luck. Knowing that Benita and Celestino were planning to come heightened my mood, and to my surprise, I was even looking forward to her wet kisses and hugs. With a four-year old's anticipation, I was anxious to open all the gifts that were still to come.

In preparation of the big day, Mother scrubbed and painted the walls with a yellow the shade of a pale rose bud. She then polished the coral and speckled cream tile floors throughout the whole house.

Father prepared as well, buying a new camel-colored gabardine suit, and Mother bought enough fabric to make a matching suit for me to wear on my special day. For herself, she sewed a floral wool circle skirt that she paired with a new high collar, long-sleeved sweater, accessorizing her look with new shoes, a belt, and Tia Cecilia's choker of cream-colored pearls.

On the day of the party, all the food had been laid out in an extravagant display. There was so much to eat: small, salty deviled ham sandwiches with finely chopped pickles inside, potato salad decorated with sliced egg and topped with pimento, chicken croquettes, tiny croissants, a fancy buttercream round cake with a ship flying a pirate's flag from its main mast. There was strawberry ice cream to serve with the cake, sodas for the children and the other guests, and of course, cold bottles of beer set aside for the men.

Father had left the house early in the morning of the party to go play dominos, but he must have lost track of time because by the time guests started to arrive, he wasn't there, and I saw how Mother's mood darkened with each second that passed as she started to pace back and forth.

Back and forth Mother paced, her anxiety building as she greeted each guest, until she stormed out the house without saying a word. Not long after, she returned with Father trailing behind. However, Benita and Celestino hadn't followed and didn't come to my birthday party that day.

Once Father had changed into his suit, Mother pushed the guests around the dining table, and with a loud exaggerated voice, asked everyone to sing *Feliz Cumpleaños* to me.

Overwhelmed by all the unfocused emotions in the room, I just wanted to run away and hide, knowing fully well that I could not because my job was to smile for each picture and perform.

When the party was over and the crowd was finally gone, after the house had been meticulously scrubbed, Mother, waiting for the ideal moment, slapped Father's face as I stood there and gasped, too frightened to cry.

ADORATION

"*La escuela quiere un niño bonito para cantar una canción.*" That is how Mother told me that because of my handsomeness, I had been selected to sing a solo about the fruits of the land during the school's end-of-year festivities. But I already knew because I had heard the teachers saying that they wanted me because of my looks and not necessarily because I could sing. In fact, singing wasn't something I had ever done for anyone. Still, they expected the four-year-old me, then in first grade, to charm the crowd with my radiant beauty, and I had begun looking forward to the adulation that was soon to come.

The preparations started with a whirlwind of activity that completely focused on me. There was a special song for me to learn. I was then taught how to stand behind a large basket to be filled with fruits and vegetables from Father's stand. I was taught the proper way to hold my arms and move my hands, when to smile and when to bow, when to exit the stage for the next act.

There were so many outfits for me to try on. Should I dress as a peasant farmhand with torn pants and sing barefoot? Should I dress in the long-sleeve gray shirt and pants that more affluent farmers wore? Unable to decide, Mother brought each outfit after school one day, making me parade for a panel of teachers while wearing each one. In the end, I wore my pants rolled up at the ankles, my shirt tied into a knot at the waist, and a field hand's hat on my head. By the evening of the show, I found myself lost in the commotion because I had been reduced to one more stage prop and I wasn't special anymore.

I refused to go on, crossing my arms and planting my feet on the floor. Infuriated, Mother pushed me out onto the stage. Blinded by the bright lights, it was hard to see the faces in the crowd. Still, I could not run backstage with Mother, the teachers and helpers blocking the way. I had no recourse but to stand there and sing. And why not sing? I had learned the song and I knew what to do. So standing behind the basket bursting with Father's produce, I sang the silly old song about the bounty of the land.

When I finished the song, I smiled and bowed, but in my silence, I became mesmerized by the roar coming from the crowd. Instead of leaving the stage, I continued to smile and bow, refusing to move despite the adults in the wings signaling to free the stage for the next act.

Hearing cheers and accolades was a new experience for me, and I loved how this attention made me feel. All at once, I existed in a wonderful daydream where everything revolved around me and no one else mattered. In a flash, I made the connection between my looks and the power they I held over everyone. This magic moment ended abruptly the second that Mother walked out onto the stage and dragged me off, kicking and screaming to let me return to the stage.

AROUSAL

It was a chilly early winter morning when Tico and I met for the first time and gazed into each other's eyes. There we both stood, face to face in front of the school, with our mothers by our sides. It was his first day there, and I remember reaching for him, taking his hand, and walking together into Raquel's happy class. His mother, with a soft smile, had encouraged him as she explained to Mother that her son was very shy. *"Mira que bien, ya encontraste un amiguito."* Look, how good, you already found a friend, she lovingly explained.

Tico was taller than me, but not by much, and his frame was small just like mine. I marveled at how his hand perfectly fit inside mine. Like his mother, his wavy hair was light brown with a touch of gold, and his glowing bronze skin made his light blue eyes shine. He was the only dark child in the class, and on that day every student that walked past slowed down and gawked as I stared then down with a frown. I did hear a teacher whisper that his mother was a maid, just as another raised her browns and wondered who his father was, but I was too young to understand. That afternoon, at home, I could not stop talking about Tico, and Mother seemed content that I, too, had found a new friend.

Not long after Tico arrived at school, a magician dressed in a vampire suit, cape, and tall hat named Mandrake came to perform. While we were at lunch, the teachers stacked all the desks in the largest classroom against the walls to create space on the floor for the students to sit. Rushing to the room, Tico and I sat side by side with our knees neatly crossed. Excited with anticipation, we laughed, giggled, squinted, and held tight to one another's hands.

In the middle of his act, the magician reached for a rabbit inside his hat. At that moment, we both guided our hands up the leg of other's shorts and rested them on each other's crotch. Flushed with this virgin sensation, I felt warm and content, no longer caring about the rabbit or the magician's hat—only that Tico's pretty eyes were smiling at me.

It all ended in a flash when the helmeted, stern teacher pulled us apart and dragged us out of the room by our arms. It all happened so fast that all anyone noticed was the magician pulling an endless string of brightly colored hankies from his tightly closed fist.

We spent hours in separate rooms and away from everyone until both of our mothers came to pick us up at the end of the day. But even then, they insisted that Mother and I wait until Tico and his mother were gone.

Nothing was said at home that night, and when I returned to school the next day, Tico wasn't in the classroom. He was nowhere to be found, but all the teachers walked away every time I asked about him.

I'd not understand until much older that when it came time for the school to decide which child should be kept and which child should be discharged, it came down to Tico's questionable parentage and the whiteness of my skin. I never saw my bronze-skinned friend again.

REJECTION

My first-grade schoolwork came quite easy to me, and learning the math tables or remembering facts were all things that I mastered after the first try. I could hear something once and easily repeat it back whenever the teacher asked.

The helmeted teacher who, to my surprise, taught the first grade, enjoyed claiming the credit for my excellence. This made me hate her even more for what she had done to Tico and me. Yet I also craved her approval and wanted her love. Wanting to make her happy, I became the first student to jump up with the correct answer every time.

Emboldened by my repeated accomplishments, I began to show off and bragged outrageously to everyone, never caring that the other kids also wanted to shine. Blind to my satisfaction, I didn't see how much they all had begun to resent who I was. It wasn't long before I found myself alone in the schoolyard at recess time.

Confused and determined to be accepted, I forced myself on the boys, self-righteously, interrupting their baseball game. I'd march up to a kid and rip the baseball or glove from their hand, which only made things worse, especially because I didn't know how to play. In return, the boys pushed me to the ground until I ran away and cried.

One day, I walked over to where Cousin Sandra was playing with the rest of the girls, but they also rejected me because boys didn't jump rope or play hopscotch. Still, I stayed by the girls because it was safer being there than being attacked.

Once, I was startled to see Father's stoic face staring at me from the other side of the fence. His brow narrowed, he examined the scene as I stood with the girls, but soon walked away without walking over to me.

When I got home that afternoon, Mother and Father reprimanded me and told me how ashamed they both were because I wanted to play with the girls rather than the boys. I tried to explain, but they refused to listen to me.

On the next day, trapped in a world where I wasn't wanted by the kids in my class, and dreading my parent's reproach, I walked to an isolated corner of the yard, picked up a stick, and began drawing in the dirt as the teachers looked on, not saying a word or doing anything.

REVENGE

I was born favoring my left hand, and at home I had been allowed to eat and draw with it. My being left-handed, everyone in the family agreed was an oddity, but Papá had been consulted and he decided that as this was how I was born, nothing needed to be done. School would not agree with his advice.

Raquel never seemed to mind, but the first-grade helmeted teacher I hated disapproved the moment she saw me holding the pencil with my left hand. Walking over to me, she unbuckled my belt, pushed my left wrist through the space between the pants and the belt, and with great force, cinched it very tightly so that it became impossible for me to free up my arm.

The first time that this happened, I showed Mother the painful welt on my wrist. This abuse stirred a great agitation in her, driving her to run to the school, dragging me by my bruised arm to complain and demand satisfaction. I silently stood there to watch Mother wilt in the chair when they informed her that such oddities where not tolerated in their school, and that although my deformity had been tolerated in the country, I was unacceptable in any decent Havana school, explaining to the peasant woman that I was using the Devil's hand and not the right hand of God:

"Pero señora, por favor, comprenda que él está usando la mano siniestra, que es la mano del Diablo. Esto no es posible aquí en esta ciudad. Estamos tratando de enseñarle a usar su mano diestra, que es la mano del Señor."

Embarrassed, Mother turned red and offered them her total support. From that moment on, every time I tried to use my left hand at home, Mother, too, threatened to strap my wrist with a belt.

Throughout the struggle, no one had listed to me. I wasn't allowed to defend myself or explain. I felt like a possession to be bartered away for the best possible price. I did not matter. All that mattered was for the family to be accepted by everyone. I had no choice but to comply, secretly focusing my anger on that teacher I had learned to hate.

I wallowed in my anger until the one day when I could no longer hold back and began using my left hand to write. Like a soaring vulture waiting to drop on its prey, the teacher was next to me in a flash, ready to tie me down with my belt again.

Taking her by surprise, I raised my Devil's hand, and with all the strength I could muster, slapped her powdered, cratered face and laughed. Everyone in class laughed with me, and then laughed at me as she dragged me to the front of the class. Forcing my hand open, palm up, she ordered me to stand still and not cry as she wielded the flat side of her wooden ruler against it until my palm bled.

But she wasn't finished with me. After grabbing me by my shirt sleeve and dragging me to the corner of the room, she pushed me down on my knees with me face to the wall. For a full hour, she stared at the clock as I knelt on hard grains of rice. When it came time to get up, my knees were bleeding as well. Mother didn't speak a single word to me when we got home that afternoon. In complete silence, she bathed me, helped me put on my pajamas, and closed my bedroom door. She never returned, not even to bring me dinner or something to drink.

Later that evening, Father quietly came into the room, placing his index finger on his lips and asking me to shush before sitting next to me and feeding me the cold rice pudding that Mother had made earlier that day.

My final punishment came at the end of the year when the school refused to enroll me for the second grade. Mother panicked at first when the news came. However, her fury soon cooled when she saw my dismissal as a personal insult. *"No te preocupes, hay muchas escuelas,"* I heard her say, bragging about how there was more than one school that I could attend.

HUMILIATION

Mother was elated the minute she heard I had been invited to Jorgito's birthday celebration—primarily because his family were the richest people on the block. He was two years older than me, and therefore not in my class at school and I had been surprised to have been invited, especially since I hated him. How could I not? With his spiky hair, squinty eyes, and a scratchy voice, Jorgito spit saliva in my face every time he spoke.

He lived down the street from us, in a newly built modern house with his parents. They even had a live-in maid. His father, our dentist, was a large, hairy man who sweated profusely, and whose enormous fingers and hands were too fat for the work he did.

Although I didn't want to go to Jorgito's birthday party, Mother saw it as an important invitation and a sign that we had been accepted by them. Mother could not have foreseen what about to come.

Our house was full of activity the week of the party. Mother made me new short black pants, a white cotton shirt, and then bought me a narrow black and white clip-on bow tie. She spent the Saturday morning of the party at the beauty parlor getting her hair and nails done. All dressed up, I sat on the edge of her bed and watched as she repeatedly checked herself out in the mirror to make sure that the seams in her stockings were straight.

Jorgito's one-story house was low to the ground, recessed back from the sidewalk, and protected on all sides by a tall wall of pale lime painted blocks. These blocks were not solid, but had an open design that allowed passersby to admire the expansive patio filled with plantings and shrubs. At a garage to the right side of the house, his father kept an enormous tail-finned, tomato-red and bright-yellow Dodge. To the left, rows of purple coleus lined the terracotta path to a front door of mint-frosted glass. The walls of the house were painted turquoise, and together with the lime, purple, orange, and green, it was an exaggerated bragging scheme that could easily be seen from each end of the block.

With our well-wrapped gift in her hand, Mother rang the doorbell only one time and the short, middle-aged maid opened the door so quickly that I was sure she had been standing on the other side waiting for us. I knew who she was. I had often seen her at Father's produce stand. She wore a pale gray uniform covered by a starched white apron. Like a ghost, she made no sound as she walked.

The great hall was flanked on both sides by large glass windows that ran from ceiling to floor. The room was so large that sofas, chairs, tables, and lamps had been easily arranged into distinct sitting areas without making the room seem overcrowded. As we stepped into the threshold, I heard Mother very quietly whisper how impressive this display of wealth was, not aware that the maid had been standing close enough to hear what she had just said.

To the right and halfway down the room was a large rectangular table overflowing with food. On the opposite wall, an angular credenza stood on skinny, round legs capped in brass, where a magnificent mountain of unwrapped toys waited for a raffle to start. Immediately, I noticed the large cordovan leather horse that stood taller than all the other toys.

All the mothers moved around in a slow, sophisticated dance while their smartly dressed children sat politely on the furniture throughout the room. Uncomfortable and nervous amidst such formality, I started to squirm until Mother forced me to sit on the edge of her chair while telling me to behave.

Once the raffle was announced, all the children were given a ticket to hold. This was followed by Jorgito's mother pulling the matching tickets from a decorated porcelain bowl.

My number was the first that she called, and I could not believe my luck when the maid handed me the beautiful cordovan horse! My joy was short lived, for a split second later, Jorgito's mother yanked the prize horse out of my hands, claiming that there had been a mistake. I burst into tears and started to cry.

"Es mi caballito. ¡Dame mi caballito!" I screamed at the top of my lungs. It is my horse. Give me my horse!

Mother stood up and demanded that I be given my prize as every woman present stared at her and rolled their eyes, and absolute silence engulfed the room. This was followed by an explosion of laughter when all the mothers, their children, and even the ghostly maid laughed.

I was still crying and begging for my horse when Mother grabbed me by the arm, ready to leave, but I refused to move without my beautiful horse. Her strength prevailed in the end, and I had no choice but to follow, not understanding what had just happened to me or why I didn't deserve to keep that beautiful cordovan horse.

We were at the front door when I heard Jorgito's mother shout: "*¡Mira a eso! ¡Que guajira tan mal educada con su diente de oro!*" Look at this! What an uneducated country peasant flashing her gold-capped tooth!

BLAME

Once we got home, Mother flew into a rage, blaming my behavior for the anguish she felt. Outraged myself, I was furious that she had claimed her pain was greater than mine. It was my horse that had been taken away, not hers!

What I longed for, even more than the horse, was for Mother to wrap her arms around me and to tell me everything would be okay, but I saw no place for me inside her pain.

The moment father came home, she sprang on him for hours, blaming his laziness for their lot in life. "*¿Por qué no buscas un trabajo bueno?*" Why are you not looking for a decent job? She kept screaming the same question, unable to stop.

That evening, after Father deciding to sleep on my old folding cot brought an end to their fights. Afterwards, all their shouting was replaced by unbearable silence and hurt.

Tía Cecilia ran away to the farm the second she saw Mother closing the blinds and keeping the usually-open front door tightly locked. No matter the hour, it was always dark in the house.

Mother cooked and kept me cleaned and dressed. She took me to school, but not to the park. She didn't stop anywhere or speak to anyone. She stayed in bed. Tears flowed from her eyes at all hours of the day and night. In the evenings, Father sat on the sofa and cried as I hid in my room, unable to cry.

Frightened and alone, like a sponge, I soaked up their emotions, tension, and pain week after week, until I cried because all the anger and pain were my fault. I cried because

I didn't know how to make everything better again. So I decided that I'd be the best son ever and obey every rule and do all that Mother asked of me without delay. I worked to impress them and charm them without any results. I became chatty and sang the tunes I had heard and mimicked the dancers that I had seen on TV. I became overly expressive, showering them with affection at every turn. None of it helped, and every night, as Mother cried alone in bed, Father stared straight ahead at the wall. I was invisible. I did not exist.

My endless attempts at injecting joy into our lives ended each day in failure, and I fell asleep alone every night with this guilt weighing on my chest.

During the months between my February birthday celebration when Mother ran out of the house, and Jorgito's September birthday celebration, our family was stranded on a roller coaster ride from hell. Everyone was stuck in a cycle of elation, euphoria, anger, and then devastation, until our home had become an unsafe house for all.

Loss

Mother and Benita's bond was never the same after my fourth birthday celebration when she dragged Father out of her house. Neither she nor Celestino attended the party that day. Sandra and her mother, who were already sitting in our living room, never entered our house again. I repeatedly asked, but none of the adults ever explained why there had been such an abrupt change in our lives.

Gone were the lazy days of playtime with Cousin Sandra. And gone were the days of visiting Benita's house. Gone was the laughter and the joy that came with each one of Benita's kisses and hugs.

In early December, Mother announced that we were moving to our new home that month, and I wished for nothing more than a chance to see Benita and Celestino one last time. I begged and begged, but no one walked me to their house, and they never came to ours to say their goodbyes.

On the day of our move, as the taxicab drove down the block past her alley, my gaze locked briefly with Benita's as she stood on the sidewalk. And for the briefest of moments, all was well again.

HOPE

On December 28, 1958, Mother, Tía Cecilia, and I rode in the back of a taxicab as bullets cracked the air overhead. In fear, the screaming women had forced me to join them as they knelt on the floor to hide. But I wasn't afraid. It was thrilling bouncing around every time the car landed on the road as it flew down a very steep hill. We were on our way to a new house and a new business that Papá had given Mother the money to buy. I could not wait to get there and for this new adventure to start, unaware that the revolution exploding all around us would bring irreversible, painful changes to our lives. I didn't know that our present good fortunes would soon turn into a future consumed by decay.

Mother's faith in this new revolution was founded on the belief that the merchant middle class that she was about to become a part of would remain just as before and be allowed to prosper and thrive. Mother didn't know how wrong she was in her hope.

Anxious, frightened, and ever more cautious, Father bolted the door to his emotions and never shared his true beliefs with anyone. Naïvely, he chose to believe that being a simple merchant working at his small produce stand made him irrelevant to the fight. And in this, he found hope.

Tía Cecilia was enthusiastic, joining the masses of people who spontaneously rushed into the streets. Gleefully, she dressed in the red and black colors of the movement and joined the multitude of believers to march along the waterfront of the *Malecón*. She even sewed a new Cuban flag to proudly fly it from the installed flagpole on the roof of our new house. Such was her hope.

I, too, had hopes. I wished for a new room with a large window through which my friends, Ms. Moon and Mr. Sun, would bathe me in their light. I hoped for our lives to return to the harmony we had briefly enjoyed after moving into our last house. Dizzy with excitement, my mind spun around and around with the promise of hope.

In every province, in every city, in every town, in every neighborhood, on every city block and every home, everyone drowned in their own hope.

FIRST DEFIANCE

My heart sank when I stepped out of the taxicab to face an ugly house with blue-gray paint peeling off its walls. It was a small, boxy one-story, flat-roofed house from where all the iron railings and its gate had been removed, just as it had been done at my school after I had refused to go in my first day of class.

Mother struggled with the three door locks, and when we walked into the living room, I gagged from the strong smell of chicken shit. A three-level metal cage crowded with loud clucking chickens fighting to claim what little space they could steal from the others, stood against the right wall—Mother's new business was already living in our house. Father was nowhere to be found, and I began looking for him.

Along a narrow hallway, there were two bedrooms and a bathroom to my right, the last bedroom emptying into a yoke-yellow dining room, and then I turned right into a maize kitchen, but Father was nowhere in sight. Crossing the open door at the back of the kitchen, I stepped into a narrow patio with a laundry sink built into a tall cement wall. To the side of the sink, a warped wooden door was held close by a brass latch. After opening it, I stepped into an enormous, cemented backyard cluttered with old furniture, a discarded sale sign, and an abandoned oil drum. On three of its sides, the patio was surrounded by a cracked and crumbling high wall. To the left of the house, a wood and chicken wire fence stood in front of a small patio belonging to the home next to us which shared a common wall with our house.

Still, Father wasn't there. So I returned to the front of the house, looking for him, this time through an inner courtyard where the equipment needed to kill and prepare the suffocating chickens stood against each wall. At the end of this inner courtyard, I stepped into a dark vestibule that measured no more than four-by-six feet. On its left sat my much-adored headboard. On my right, my old folding cot had returned. I froze in a panic as I tried to convince myself that there was a room I had missed. But I knew this was no more than a child's hide-and-seek game where he pretends that no one can see him while hiding in plain sight. In this new house, there was a bedroom for Tía Cecilia, and a bedroom for Mother and Father, but not a bedroom for me.

Bewildered, I marched into the living room where Mother and Tía were locked in conversation, threw myself on the floor and cried. I remained there until Tía helped me to my feet, almost as an afterthought, not saying anything.

Where is Father? I asked, but I didn't get a reply as the women continued to talk. Then my sadness turned to rage as I repeatedly asked where Father was and demanded to be taken to my bedroom at once.

With fear in her eyes, Tía took a few steps back while Mother stared me down with the same commanding look that she had used to frighten me in the past. But this time, I didn't move or look away. Instead, I stared back, intoxicated with the power of challenging her for the very first time in my life.

Reacting to my defiance, Mother softened her approach, and in a surprisingly maternal manner, explained that sacrifices needed to be made for the family to get ahead. Baffled by my misfortune, I struggled to understand why the sacrifice was only asked of me and not them.

"*¡Te odio!*" I hate you! I screamed in a wild yell, before running down the narrow hallway again, all the way to the dirty backyard. In frustration, I looked around for a place to hide and crawled under the old table, pushing my back against the cracks on the wall.

Father eventually showed up, but only to stand in front of me with a belt in his hand. Frightened by this new act of his, I silently followed him into the house I already despised. Once in front of the women, I refused to apologize, despite the warning of his belt. Crossing my arms over my chest, I held my ground until Tía burst into laughter, and Mother laughed when Tía pointed out that I had been acting as stubbornly as she. And with that, there was an end to the fight, with my understanding that it was possible to stand my ground and win, and that if I stood my ground, I could do as I liked.

FILTH

Mother's new *pollería* was a commonplace, smelly, and feather-filled place where live chickens were killed, plucked, gutted, and cut up to fulfill each customer's unique wish. And since she also sold eggs, it was a profitable venture because people shopped for these food staples every day.

At first, the beheaded chickens were dipped into a tub filled with boiling water to soften their feathers. After that, they were held against a spinning drum studded with long rubber fingers that quickly plucked the feathers away. After this task was completed, the chickens were briefly dipped into another hot water tub tinted with saffron. This was followed by a quick dip into a barrel of chilly water to make them look fat and bursting with plump flesh the color of corn. As such, Mother's chickens looked healthy, and as her reputation grew, the crowds of eager customers grew larger and larger on our porch and living room. From morning until late afternoon, when the store finally closed, my vestibule room was no more than the passageway between the front of the store and the chicken-dismantling inner courtyard.

Every evening, dripping barrels of wet feathers, heads, and guts passed right by my cot on their way to the edge of the road. Every night, I listened to the chickens fighting for space while the men on the loud garbage truck emptied the barrels and tossed them onto the sidewalk at the front of the house.

Every dawn, Father took me away seconds before the working men arrived to roll the sticky, smelly barrels past my bed, leaving a foul odor behind.

A Cracked Bowl

I stepped outside of our house expecting this new world to be the same as what I had previously known. But this wasn't what waited for me.

Unlike before, there were no pristine houses to pass by and admire during afternoon walks. There were no angular mid-century houses all brightly painted in peacock, flamingo, and gold.

In this new neighborhood, endless narrow alleys ran parallel to the few street-facing houses and multi-story apartment dwellings—all looking like old, bewildered beasts begging for attention and love.

On this new two-way street of constant traffic, the exhaust from the cars, buses, and trucks made the air taste like a stew that had fermented or soured after being left unattended for hours in the heat of the sun.

Daring to cross the busy street by myself, I scurried down the block to discover a bodega, and I felt happy at last because it reminded me of the bodega in our old neighborhood. I had always been fascinated by that bodega, eagerly standing by to watch its great metal walls rolling up in the morning, down for lunch, back up in the early afternoon, and finally down again at night. And how I enjoyed greeting the workers going in and out through that very tiny door built into one of the great walls. This store owner was named Fernando. He was a tall but round, jolly man with coal-black eyes and a comical mustache. From my first visit, he offered me sodas and sweets, which I ate and drank in a flash.

Just as Father did at his produce stand, Fernando catered to the women who frequented his shop. But these women were not like the educated shoppers I knew. They seemed like a wild tribe who loudly demanded to be serviced at once. Never taking a single breath, they constantly gossiped about everything and everyone, before returning home to their stoves.

Mother called them *chusma*—Cuban slang for low class—but they were the same women who shopped at our store, so she was friendly to their face. In private, she bragged about us being better than them. Only then did I stop being afraid whenever I watched one of their fights.

Just as the men did at Benita's house, the neighborhood men gathered at the bodega around a square folding table to watch other men play dominos until their turn to play came. And just as the store closed every day for lunch, they too stopped playing at midday to go home for food and a nap before returning in the early afternoon to continue their game.

But something was different about them as well, for they too were as loud as the women and spoke just as much with their whirling arms and hands as with their mouths. These men didn't dress in their best Sunday suits or their freshly starched white linen shirts to play, as Father and the men at Benita's always did. Rather, they wore their wrinkled, unbuttoned short-sleeve shirts over sleeveless tee shirts, while others wore no shirts at all. These unshaven men who never seemed to work, as Father worked, didn't smell of clean brilliantine as he did, or Old Spice as Papá did, but of coffee, tobacco, and run.

And unlike the men at Benita's house, who always allowed me to be near them and watch, these men pushed me away and looked at me as if they knew some secret that I didn't yet understand. Still, being there made me feel close to something that Father loved, and I stayed there every day after school, ignoring their unwelcoming stances while waiting for Father to come home at night.

Just as it had always been in school, the boys on the block also saw something in me that they didn't like, and refused to have me join in their games. But unlike before, the girls on the block turned me into their newly found pet, which only made the boys more jealous and angrier toward me. Unlike in school, when the boys simply pushed me away, these boys dealt with their feelings by beating me up and forcing me back into the house.

FIRST CRUSH

Mother hired Miguel in January 1959, just days after we had moved to our new house. I first met him one afternoon, after the van had dropped me off since I was still attending the first grade at my old school. He was standing behind the counter on my left and partly hidden by the scale and cash register. I took one look at him and could not move. Instead, I stared at him with such intensity that his milky face turned bright red, and he felt the need to lower his peridot eyes.

Unaware of our brief exchange, Mother took me over to him, and when he shook my hand, a shock of electricity ran up and down my spine. Frightened by this new experience that I didn't understand, I ran all the way to the back of the house and hid in the backyard. He was sixteen, and I was to turn five in a month.

From that moment on, Miguel, and not Mother, cared for me, and it was his job to walk with me to the park every afternoon after I had washed and changed into my play clothes.

We seldom exchanged a single word during our outings to the park. I didn't care. It never bothered me because I was happy just holding his hand. This tall and muscular man made me feel safe without saying anything. His familiar quietness reminded me that Father, too, was a quiet man.

By the start of classes the next year, Mother had convinced a different school just five blocks away from our house to let me skip the second grade. This was important to her not only because it proved that my old school had been wrong in dismissing me, but also because it was something she could brag about to everyone. On and on she went, bragging about how her son was skipping grades, as she once did. In fact, I was happy knowing that I didn't have to face the nasty helmeted teacher again. I was happy just running away.

I was very happy with this change because it meant that Miguel was going to walk me there in the morning and pick me up at the end of the day. However, this didn't come to be, for Mother insisted that I was old enough to go there and back on my own. She also informed me that, being five years old, I was old enough to walk to the park on my own. This brought an end to my happy walks with Miguel. Even so, I saw Miguel every morning and every afternoon, and I found reasons to hang around the store and stare at him. Everyone loved Miguel, but not as much as I did.

FIRST FRIEND

Tía Cecilia married Tío Patrício in October 1961. With a thinning hair line, a bushy mustache, and deepset eyes, this lanky man could have never been labeled as handsome, but in a suit and tie, he seemed refined to me. Calm and uncomplicated, his presence was soothing and his disposition warm. Tía Cecilia and Tío Patricio formed a perfect unit that existed happily without others in their lives, living intertwined as if a pair of Lladró figurines purposely designed to be sold as a set.

Patrício wasn't a man with an official education, but from him, I learned much about history and literature—Victor Hugo, Cervantes, and even Balzac. He taught me the stories of the Borgia and the Medici families, and of the Italian Renaissance. Some of his history lessons were factual and some imagined, but I relished the stories just the same, happily indulging his habit for telling tall tales in the same manner that Celestino always used to.

He could talk for hours about antiquity, Ancient Rome, and Greek mythology. It was his excitement over these subjects that made me want to learn about the gods: Zeus or Jupiter; Aphrodite or Venus; Poseidon or Neptune; blond Apollo, whom I wanted to be; even Hades or Pluto, the god of the Underworld, a place Patrício tried to explain to me, but I didn't understand.

It was his love for such things that made me fall in love with history, instilling in me a lifelong desire to read and explore.

Behind his outward calmness breathed a passionate artist and entertainer who expressed his love for me by the care he took to weave the stories he told. Once, he spun a tale about Pope Joan, who had been discovered to be a woman. Patrício would then explain how the enclave of cardinals commissioned a large chair of pure gold and encrusted with gleaming jewels and stones from where the bottom had been removed. He would go on to explain that every time a new papal candidate was named, he had to sit in this chair, lift his vestments, and allow all the other cardinals to reach under it and check. Chanting *"Huevos tenemos, papa seremos,"* each cardinal having touched the candidate's testicles, confirmed his qualification to be Pope.

Once Father started spending his days and nights elsewhere for extended periods of time, Tío Patrício tried to fill the void as the man of the house. However, Mother didn't welcome this and soon made it clear that it was her house, insisting that everyone in it had to live by her rules, clearly making the point that she'd raise me as she saw fit. So no matter what he witnessed or heard, he was never to criticize what she did or said. *"Nadie aquí me dice cómo se supone que debo criarlo."* No one here tells me how I'm supposed to raise my own son.

Mother's rules built a wall between *los tíos* and me from the start, forcing me to live at the peripheries of their lives. Within the formality that Mother demanded of him, Tío Patrício signaled his care by sharing his stories with me. Still, I knew not to pay him too much attention when Mother was around, and I knew it was best for everyone if I kept at a distance from him.

FIRST TEMPTATION

Mother didn't allow me to be friends with Sebastián, the small fourteen-year-old orphan boy from Spain who lived with his aunt in the house attached to our house. She said that they were poor, and that we didn't know anything about them. She said that there was a reason for the tall chicken wire fence separating their small backyard from our large backyard, but that didn't make any sense to me. What reason could there be? Their own small yard on the other side of the fence was clean and much neater than ours was.

At first, 1 told myself that 1 didn't care about what she said, given that from the moment of our move, Mother had been too busy running the store to notice what 1 was doing or where 1 was at any given time. Besides, 1 was quickly becoming accustomed to do as 1 liked since the day of our move when 1 first stood up to her. Yet 1 understood her temper and thought it was best for me to stay on my side of the fence whenever 1 played in our backyard. Regardless of the distance 1 kept, there was something fascinating about this boy whose skin was so pale that 1 could see the pulsating blood right under it whenever he blushed. His red hair glowed like gold in the sun.

For my fifth birthday that year, Father gave me four guinea pigs and built a large pen for them. He told me that cleaning after them and feeding them was my responsibility alone. 1 happily spent hours after school, feeding and caring for them. By early spring, Father needed to enlarge the pen repeatedly because a new litter kept arriving each month.

As part of my caring duties, Father took me to the two produce stands near our house and made a deal for me to stop by every afternoon after school and take away their discarded bits of wilted lettuces, damaged cabbage leaves, broken celery, carrots—anything that would have been swept away at the end of the day. This was the first job I ever had, and I took it seriously, always making sure their pen was neat, and that they were hydrated and fed.

I remember feeling pride over something I alone had done, which Father rewarded by saying that I was on my way to becoming a big boy, even though I wasn't sure at all what he meant. I spent many happy hours before and after school in the backyard, playing and doing my job.

From his side of the fence, Sebastián liked tinkering within all sorts of things while wearing nothing except his cotton underwear shorts. Every time I was out in my yard, he too would come out and try to get my attention by asking me what I was doing and crying out my name in the voice of a cat: "*Miau, Martincito, miau,*" he'd say. *Misu, misu,* calling me over as if I was also a cat.

At first, I refused to look at him and pretended to be occupied with my work, but I was in fact intrigued by him. I could not stop looking at his body shimmering in the afternoon summer heat. This game of mine was no more than a waste of time because I never could resist him in the end, and it always ended with me walking over to my side of the fence to watch him rub his stomach and chest up and down until his hand disappeared into his shorts. Our game continued with me pushing my small hand though the six-sided holes in the wire fence to rub the fine rust-colored hair on his stomach and chest, only to quickly pull my hand back. As when Tico and I had reached into each other's short pants, me putting my hand on Sebastián's body made me feel all warm and content.

INVASION

only remember the Bay of Pigs invasion as flickering black and white flashes on our TV. Confused, I watched the captured invading men walking on the beach with hands locked behind their necks.

I remember sitting next to Father and trying to follow the tribunal hearings where these men were interrogated and then publicly forced to repent. But I didn't understand; I was a child.

What I remember the most is eating peanut butter for the first time out of that one small blue-labeled jar that Mother got at the bodega after these men had been exchanged for food and medicine.

HUNGER

Food rationing came early in 1962, and the great cages in our living room which had always been filled with chickens, emptied overnight. Live chickens were delivered, if luck would have it, once a week, along with the allotted number of eggs that the store was granted to sell, but these things didn't always arrive as planned.

In the uncertainty of the months and years to come, people took to forming a neighborhood watch in front of every store, staying there from morning until it was clear that no new deliveries would arrive that day. When one did, the neighborhood watchers would fan out in all directions, spreading the extraordinary news. Shortly to follow was a hectic whirlwind of customers in front of the one lucky store.

In front of our house, they pushed and shoved, each person maneuvering to get in front of the line—*al frente de la cola.* This was important since no one ever knew how many chickens had been delivered on that fortunate day. It never mattered in the end since there were never enough chickens for everyone, and as soon as the last of the chickens was sold, Mother rushed to send the disappointed customers away while nervously closing the door to our house.

Outside, the hungry, angry people, gesturing wildly with their hands and arms, argued and shouted at each other without stop.

Just as fast, the blocks' revolutionary committee would show up to remind the crowd that Cuba had no food shortages, and then the fighting mob was replaced by a procession of sad people walking back to their house.

The ones that dared to linger behind scared me the most because I feared that they might turn violent and push their way into the house. So I took to running out to the backyard and hiding from them.

In their hunger, I could hear them accuse Mother of having lied and of hiding some of the chickens from them. And of course, I knew she had, because Mother always managed to save a few chickens for us and the staff.

The staff ran the risk of being caught while taking their illegal portions with them. So they waited until the committee members were out of sight before leaving the house. To be safe, Mother outfoxed then by cutting the chickens into small pieces that could easily be concealed in a folded newspaper that the workers could casually tuck under their arm.

In this regulated world, families were forced to use a small, complicated ration book when buying any goods. These books were filled with pages and pages listing every item that each woman, man, and child was allowed to have. People could buy milk, but only if their qualifications matched. Parents could buy toys for their children, but only until their fourteenth birthday arrived.

This new world created a fertile ground for the ingenious and crooked Cuban merchants to thrive. Cleverly, they recorded the allowed amount in the people's ration books, but with the swiftest of hands, they held back a little from the people they disliked and gave it to those that they liked.

Mother embraced this game with open arms, determined to be the most powerful merchant on the block. Unaware that everyone was onto her game, she took others to be fools. She mistook their flattery as a sign of victory, thinking that she once again had pulled the wool over their eyes. *"Ay Margarita, que linda tu estás hoy,"* they'd say to her, appealing to her vanity by complimenting the beauty of her face.

All this chaos came with an unexpected change when the government closed Father's small neighborhood stand and forced his customers to shop at stores blocks away from their homes.

Set adrift, he was left with little do. To make matters worse, Mother stubbornly refused to turn the running of her store over to him, thus relegating him to the lowly position of a hired hand.

Tía Cecilia tried to intercede, reminding Mother that a man needed to feel that he had a purpose within his own house. But she would have none of it, for the house was in her name, and she had single-handedly built the business from scratch.

Embarrassed by a wife he could not keep in line, and angry that she had dethroned him as head of the family, it didn't take long before Father began to disappear for days at a time.

Gone forever were the days of pleasant mothers, maids, and grandmothers casually shopping at his produce stand. And gone were the spirited conversations between Father and the men who stopped by to chat. Gone as well were all my hopes for returning to the old neighborhood to visit Sandra, Benita, or Celestino. Why return when it only reminded Father of all that he had lost?

Those times had vanished into some dreamlike past that would never return, because the revolution had turned our lives into something that was dirty and dark, leaving us angry and sad.

BLOCKADE

I'm certain about the things I clearly remember, even today, about the missile crisis and the naval blockade.

I know that taking the bus and walking up to the *Malecón* to gaze into the horizon, hoping to spot a patrolling American battleship, became everyone's favorite pastime. I remember being there, but not who was with me. I'm not sure that I ever saw any of the ships, despite everyone in the crowd swearing they did—the power of a shared dream that allowed everyone see what they wanted to see.

I know I filled with excitement on those nights when the power went out and I could hear the low-flying planes passing overhead. I felt giddy whenever I escaped out into our porch in the dark. From there, I could see the bright bullets flying out of the artillery guns placed on the roofs of the tall buildings all around our house.

Once, I ran up and down in joy, showing everyone the unspent bullet that I had found in the middle of our backyard. Then I felt anger when Mother took the bullet from my hand and said that I could not share my secret with anyone.

Most of all, I enjoyed playing the game that one night, when the fighting seemed so close that Mother and Tía Cecilia took a hold of my hand and we all crawled under a bed to hide. How I laughed nonstop when, in the rush to get under the bed, Mother stumbled and brought down the box spring and mattress on top of everyone.

ADVENTURE

As a child, I was the happiest whenever a new venture was about to start, and I welcomed each of them with endless anticipation and hope, always curious about the unknown and ready to interact with the world.

My first-grade school trip with Tía Cecilia to Viñales, the most beautiful valley in the world, remains the first expedition that I recall.

I remember the day-long trips to the beach, where I could secretly lust after the beautiful young men as the saltwater glistened against their chiseled, tanned chests.

There were the joyous moments when I rode the brightly painted traveling carousel erected on the empty lot a block from our house. And God, how I can still feel the excitement of reaching for the brass ring prize time after time.

But nothing—not even the salt-kissed young men—could match the exhilaration of riding the Ferris wheel and roller coaster at the big amusement park, with Tío Patrício by my side.

No matter the thrill of any escapade, I'd always be the happiest during my trips to see Papá and Mamá, my maternal grandparents, and stay with them at their comfortable farm. I loved my life there because it was the one place where no one ever bullied me, and no man ever desired me. I began my life on the farm and returned to it as often as I could. The farm represented everything that was happy and safe.

I do not know why it is that my earliest complete memory of such trips comes from 1960, when I was six, years before the revolution took it all away and forever changed our lives. I remember every preparation, every detail, every smell, every taste, every emotion I felt.

The Chariot
and its Prince

The cool morning greeted Father and me the moment we went outside to welcome the hired chauffeur who was taking us to the farm. At first, I could not take my eyes off the sleek 1959 Impala because its massive set of folding fins made me believe that it wasn't a car, but a mythical bird ready to soar in flight.

Then my attention shifted when I saw Rolando get out of the car. I held my breath as I stared at that tall, lanky man holding a cigarette in his left hand. All I wanted to do was sit in the front seat next to him, and not in the back seat as Mother was expecting me to do.

Sheepishly, I whispered my wish into Father's ears, begging him to let me sit next to him, but he was fearful, reminding me that it was best not to upset Mother at the start of our drive. "¡Mira! Ya sabes cómo se pone." Look! You know how she gets, was his reply.

I would not relent, and instead flew through the car's open front door and made myself small on the seat and didn't pop up until Mother, by then already sitting in the back seat, called me to get in. However, it was too late for me to sit out back because Rolando had already pulled away from the curb.

Content with the results, I sat in the middle of the front seat with my right hand on Father's thigh, as I always did when sitting next to him, and my left hand on the thigh of my newly found prince.

GREEN

At first, the drive took us through busy city blocks, until reaching the wide Vía Blanca, when the restrained car creature was at last ready to fly along the pale celadon waves gently reaching the shores of white sand. Then, as the road began to rise away from the coast, we arrived at the majestic Bacunayagua Bridge, floating high above the land.

Jumping over Father to be near the window and get a better look, my gaze danced from one royal palm tree to the next, entranced by the erectness of their silvery trunks and the mellow swaying of their emerald tops.

"*¡Para! ¡Para!*" I screamed, asking Rolando to stop the car in the middle of the busy road, convinced that I could touch them by getting out of the car and reaching out with my hand. He humored me by slowing down as everyone laughed. "*¡Dios mío, qué niño!*" Tía Cecilia cried—Dear God, what a child!

Not long after passing the great bridge and the old town hugging the beautiful bay, we plunged south and then east along the narrow Carretera Central, and then the landscape morphed as we left the mountains behind. Ahead, sugar cane grew rich and tall while cotton gauze unfolded across unending azure skies.

Sacred *Ceiba* trees spread their roots through the land like magical dragons stretching their wings to warm themselves in the sun. *Flanboyan* trees showed off their branches bursting with flower clusters of pineapple yellow, vermilion, and deep marigold. *Madreselva* draped across barriers and fences, their sweet-scented blossoms all painted in shades of pale butter and summer corn.

Lazy grazing cows looked up at us while silently chewing their cud. *Guajiros* rhythmically bounced up and down on their horses while riding the narrow paths at the edge of the road. Red earth country lanes led to *bohíos* and *aldeas,* which greeted us and quickly disappeared as soon as we passed.

Every now and then, a small town welcomed us, sometimes to our left, and others to our right, all offering a chance to stop for fresh *agua de coco* or sweet plump *mandarinas,* which were always braided into juicy garlands of delight. Once, at one of our stops, I saw a fern feathered parrot stretch its cyan wings as it balanced itself on top of a fruit seller's hat. As far as my eyes could see, everything was living and bright.

These brief joyful memories from that happy ride are the gifts that God, on that day, planted in my heart. I call on them still and sit surrounded by the infinite shades of green that have remained so vivid throughout my life. In this space, I take shelter, and in its calmness, my soul finds repose.

Far Away Dreams

T he sun coming through the windshield of the car felt hot on my skin when the Carretera Central began slicing through the town. It was a large but still walkable town—a *pueblo* aspiring to be an important *ciudad*—and there, Mother's side of the family had built a compound away from the farm.

The car pulled up in front of the corner house where *los abuelitos*, Mother's paternal grandparents, lived. Two doors down, Papá and Mamá had also built a house, but it would sit empty until August 1965.

By intuition, or by chance, *los abuelitos* were sitting on their porch as if waiting for us to arrive, and their greetings, handshakes, kisses, and hugs were genuine and bursting with familiar love. However, what I remember most from that moment was the amber saliva drooling down Abuelito's gray stubbles as he chewed his tobacco. When he smiled, his teeth were brown and cracked.

More conversation followed, and after lunch, we settled in for a midday nap. I tried, but I wanted to explore rather than sleep, and when the opportunity came, I snuck out of the kitchen door at the back of the house and scurried down the courtyard until reaching the back door of the dark living room. The front window's blinds were tightly closed to block the intense heat and bright midday sun. Tobacco spittoons stood guard by each corner of the room. A deep brown wooden settee and two matching chairs seemed uncomfortable and too big for the small space. But what intrigued me the most were the brightly colored pictures covering the walls.

One of then illustrated a twisted tree and walls of flowers in front of which three chatting ladies sat at the edge of a smooth silvery pool. In another picture, a mischievous naked boy leaned over a smiling young woman as she stretched herself on the ground at the edge of a still, violet lake. Behind her were lush green trees and gilded jeweled mountains, all bathed in bright morning sunlight.

Wanting to join in, I emulated her and stretched out on the living room floor and smiled at the naked boy who smiled back. Happy in each other's company, we all took a nap.

ROSE WATER RAIN

T he sun sliced through the back window of the car as we left *los abuelitos* and began driving east once again. Ahead of us in the far distance, gray and purple clouds rolled by. They were the type of broken clouds where walls of sunlight cut through the rain to caress the land. *"La hija del diablo se está casando"*—the devil's daughter is getting married—is what Father said when I pointed at them and asked.

There was no warning on where to turn except a small sign by the side of the road, announcing the town's name and pointing to a narrow road ahead. The red earth of the earlier fields had by then morphed into a deep brown which gently gave way to the lane's chalky tan clay.

Forward we rolled down the scruffy Main Street and past the courthouse where Mother and Father had wed, until we stopped in front of the lime-green house at end of the town's last block.

The creamy-blue front door of the house was flanked by short, shuttered windows. There was no sidewalk to step out onto, and the street's mix of brown earth and clay was soft and muddy under my orthopedic black boots. The air smelled clean, as if the recent brief showers had given the town and the house a well-needed bath.

An old, but still handsome, woman wearing a white apron and a pale-yellow cotton frock opened the door. Abuela, my paternal grandmother, greeted everyone in a distinct *guajira* welcoming chant.

Everyone could smell the freshly brewed *café* that was waiting, and Rolando came in as well, for it would have been impolite for him to refuse. He had grown up with Father, and to Abuela, he was one of her sons.

As we entered, Abuela freely granted praises, along with robust hugs and kisses, to each one of us. Thus, Tía Cecilia held back, as she constantly did, always more comfortable when keeping a distance than when returning affections received.

Pretending to ignore her discomfort, Abuela continued to move down the line while leaving a faint scent of rose water behind, and for the first time for me, life had become a joyful whisper in time.

HARMONY

The floors of the house were smooth gray cement, and all the walls had been painted bright blue. The inner walls that separated the rooms were slightly taller than a man and only reached as high as the unpainted beams that ran throughout the house. The roof, covered in interwoven dried palm leaves that protected the house, was supported by rafters that shot high to create a sharp summit top.

Excited to be in her company, the adults talked all at once as we gathered around the glossy blue rectangular kitchen table as Abuela poured coffee in everyone's cup. Bore with the grownups chatter, I scanned the room, soaking up every detail of her kitchen, where she was most at home catering to everyone.

A beaten Dutch door next to an old charcoal-burning stove led to the garden outback. There were open shelves filled with crockery, dishes, and pots. A rotund butterscotch-colored clay jar filled with sweet, cold water from the well just outside, sat on top of a sturdy wooden stand. A dented and cratered tin lid protected the water from the flies and a small, chipped white enamel communal drinking cup sat upside down atop the tin lid. The late afternoon's amber light breaking through the opened upper half of the Dutch door bathed the room in a golden glow until overtaken by the evening's gray dusk. It was then that the kerosene lamps were brought out and placed strategically throughout the house.

Mesmerized by the spirals of smoke curling out of the top of its thick, curved glass, I sat staring at the lamp on our table until all the chatter and noise had faded away and all I heard was the hissing of the flames. Time stilled and my heart joined the snake of smoke and the lion-faced flames in their dance.

Anguish

I was sitting next to Tía Cecilia when El Viejo staggered into the room. After pushing me aside, he wrapped his arm around my aunt. Scowling from the smell of rum on his breath, her rabbit eyes, inherited from Mamá, shot Father a look as her face flushed. Abruptly, Father stood to challenge the old man, who quickly walked away. Father followed, pushing him forward as to make sure he could not turn back.

The sounds of chair legs scraping the cement floor or banging against one another, echoed from the living room until Father slammed the front and bolted it for the night. Not a word was said about the incident when he returned to the kitchen. In silence, the women cleared dishes from the table as the meal had end abruptly. "*¿Que pasó?*" I asked, but no one answered me. Instead, Mother escorted me out and into the bedroom on the other side of the wall to undress and change me into my sleeping clothes, all the while insisting I be quiet and promise to sleep the entire night.

As undecipherable voices traveled from over the shared wall late into the night, I silently sobbed into my pillow, alone in the dark.

ENCHANTED RIDE

The hot morning sun had dried up the muddy ground, allowing for wispy dust clouds to guide our path to the train depot not too far from Abuela's house. In the humid heat, stained-glass-winged dragon flies hovered and then darted about while delicate white and yellow butterflies flew close to the ground, searching for moisture and salt.

Little was discussed that morning at breakfast, and I, a bit choked-up, had difficulty swallowing my food. Unlike her warm welcome the previous afternoon, Abuela appeared sad, and her kisses were tinted with a serious tone as she stood by the door and said goodbye.

Holding my hand, Father walked me down past the fruit processing plant right before the train depot. The rich smell of guava, papaya, and sour orange syrupy sweets that were bring packed into brightly labeled oblong tins and fat round cans infused the air, the taste of which lingered on my tongue.

A tiny, whitewashed building with faded blue trim waited for us on the other side of the tracks. There, two simple wood benches huddled against the mud-covered walls to welcome Mother, Tía Cecilia, and our luggage, while Father and I went in to visit with the men. Inside, the dark, cool interior, a gangly man paced back and forth behind a long counter, selling cigarettes, cigars, sodas, beer, and small glasses of rum.

Father sat me on top of the counter and began introducing me to the men at the bar, until the urgent klaxon alerted us to the arrival of our ride. In a hurry, we downed the cold citrusy *salutaris* we were sharing through a red-striped paper straw. Outside, an amazing contraption waited for us.

Little more than a rudimentary wooden bus built on top of a freight rail car, our *guaguita* was red with a noisy engine spewing white smoke. There were two open doors—one at the back, and one on the side with a short ladder for riders to step up into the car. It being high off the ground required Mother and Tía Cecilia to hold their skirts down as they climbed. Luckily, that morning they had changed from their high-heels into bright rubber flip-flops—Mother's were fuchsia pink, and Tía Cecilia's were mint. Always coordinated and anticipating such a moment, they even lacquered their toenails to match the nail color on their hands.

Sitting on a small *taburete* that had been nailed to the wooden floor, Candela, the rotund, jovial driver, oozed from either side. My eyes bulged upon hearing Father explain the reason for his name, because it meant a burning flame. But when he laughed and assured me there was nothing to fear, I relaxed. Still, I played it safe, keeping one eye on Candela's every action until my attention focused elsewhere once we started to move away from the train depot.

Inside, a row of long narrow benches on each side stretched the length of the car. Above the seats, rows of glassless windows displayed flapping canvas shades helplessly trying to block the insistent hot sun. Its ceiling was low, forcing the adults to hunch over when they entered or stood.

Once in motion, passengers bounced about on their seats, wobbling up and down and side by side. Then, as the *guaguita* picked up speed, the recurring thuds from the wheels against the joints on the track lulled the passengers into a trance. But for me, there was too much to see. Well-worn men smiled through tanned and wrinkled faces as their large hands held onto their woven palm leaf hats. Delighted to be in familiar territory again, Father eagerly engaged them in a discussion about the harvest and their hopes for the better life that the revolution had promised to every laboring man.

Friendly women wore canvas shoes with laces and simple cotton dresses as they held tightly onto small children who stared at our big-city paleness and my red and black cowboy shirt. But unlike Father, Mother and Tía Cecilia only nodded politely, content talking to each other and no one else.

My heart ready to burst, I gazed at the endless countryside flying by in front of me. I belonged there; I wasn't a separate being.

There were no mountains or hills on my land, but acres of flat green fields that stretched everywhere on either side of the tracks. Large sugar cane fields were evenly tall except for the places where the harvest had been started and left behind deep and wide paths.

Every so often, the fields of green and sugar cane parted, giving way to small clusters of building and shacks shaded by coconut, avocado, and other life-giving trees—places where prancing roosters, hens, ducks, and turkeys patrolled the yards. Often, a nursing caw stood calmly tied to a spike hammered deep into the ground near the owner's house. Barefoot children skipped and jumped about while their mother's hung wash out to dry.

Hearing the change to the engine's roar, I turned around and sat next to Father again when the *guaguita* began to slow down as we approached the ancient sugar mill. There, we switched to a secondary track to clear the line for the magnificent and fierce sugar cane train to pass.

Standing on the seat for a better view as Father held me by my waist, I delighted in the sight of the enormous black locomotive passing in front of us. Polished to a shine, with smoke billowing from its stack, its enormous wheels, pistons, and gears pumped hard to pull its endless number of rail cars, each overflowing with an abundant gift from the land. In a gesture of delight, Father smiled and patted my head, just as he had done while sitting on my bed when I was three—right after Tía Nereida had taken Mother away to the farm.

The mill was an unpredictably busy place which buzzed with people waiting, departing, or switching *guaguitas* also parked on the jumble of tracks. Straight and confident atop their fine leather saddles, affluent riders dressed in gray long-sleeved shirts and matching pants. Holding firmly to the stirrups as they rode, their enormous machetes hung from the left side of their belts, ready to be brandished with the hand of God. In sharp contrast, the less prosperous farmers rode their ungallant horses while poor peasants got around on their mules or simply walked.

Pulled by huge tan *bueyes,* overloaded *carretas* maneuvered to be next at the sugar mill line. The scent from the boiling sugar cane juice reminded me of how hungry I was, and when I told Father, he promised that *la finca* wasn't far. Hungry and tired, I could not wait for the *guaguita* to start moving again.

It was then, as I looked around in inpatient misery, that a slender young man with brilliant blue eyes caught my sight. Sitting atop his shiny golden mare, he, accompanied by a strong *moreno* on a coal-colored horse, rode up to our side of the car.

All smiles, Father asked if I remembered my Uncle Nenico and Benita's brother Antonio, who worked with him at Abuela's and El Viejo's old farm.

But even before I could ask Father if they were there to take us with them, Candela blew the klaxon, revved the engine, and we slowly started to move away from the two handsome young men on horseback, the mill, the train, the lively people, and the taste of cooked sugar cane.

Fixated on his beautiful face, I reached for Nenico's hand, but Mother, who had been merrily chatting with Tía Cecilia while keeping an eye on the men, yanked my arm back just as my uncle's and my fingers touched. Disappointed, I stared at her, my face rigid with rage.

The mill faded into the distance as we chugged on down the track, passing endless fields of sugar cane once again, but not as many homesteads.

Unable to forget Nenico and Antonio, I searched the landscape for them, hoping to spot the two racing the *guaguita* to catch up with us. No matter how hard I looked, they were nowhere to be found. Eventually, at Father's insistence, I sat down on the seat next to him.

Comfortable leaning into Father's side, and with the hum of the engine keeping time, I drifted off to sleep and didn't wake up until Candela tooted the klaxon once again, revved the engine to climb the incline ahead, then applied the brakes to bring the us to a full stop, announcing, "¡*Ya llegamos!*"— We arrived!

Father helped me to my feet, giving me a chance to spin and dance. Imagining myself a bird in flight, I stretched out my arms and flapped my hands when Candela lifted me up and twirled me before handing me to Father, already on the ground waiting for me. Taking my hand, he walked me to a very tall gate built into a towering fence that stretched in either direction for as far as I could see. A willowy pine tree that had grown to be a part of the fence offered us shade as I waited for Father to open the gate. The great house stood at the end of a smooth stone path.

To our left, the wide, black earth yard reached far to the paddock's fence where a milking cow and Father's old horse were kept. As tall as trees, an endless garden of zinnias lined the stone path.

When I saw Papá and Mamá in the opening of the Dutch door, I broke away and bolted to the house. Happy to see me, he mussed my hair and hugged me close. Him being a short man, I wrapped by arms around his hips. Then, with me standing on the toe of his boots, he walked me into the house.

CITADEL

After lunch, while the others napped, I slipped out of the house and headed to the zinnia forest that had guided us along the path. The pink, orange, and fuchsia faces of the sunshine flowers watched over me as I wove in, out, and through them. Some had a single row of petals. Some had multiple rows, and some produced a whole round ball of blossoms. Gingerly, I ran my hand over the circle of tiny yellow star-shaped flowers in their center, sprouting from guava marmalade hearts.

After walking for a while, I had somehow circled the wilderness and ended up where I started to stand again on the path. I stood there for an infinity, admiring the beautiful long house.

The single-story structure was capped with a peaked woven palm leaf roof. Its outer walls framed by wood planks, the first two rows of which were painted a deep shade of mint. Above, the house was painted a pale buttercup. Tall windows with evenly spaced vertical iron bars, keeping away wild animals and unknown interlopers alike. A porch wrapped around the front and side of the house, and was covered in concave and convex waves of Spanish tiles the color of ripened tomato flesh. A climbing Jasmine that ran wild along the low, sloping roof greeted me the moment I set foot onto the porch. Lingering in its shade, I stood perfectly still to watch a hummingbird flittering from one blossom to the next. On its heavier branches, vocal finches sang their melodies while showing off their olive jackets and bright-yellow ruffs.

I followed the lilies of the valley that ran along the edge of the porch, but didn't venture into Mamá's garden that day. Instead, I returned to the cool great hall, happy, thinking that the rafters high above had bribed the brazen humidity to rise.

The brilliantly polished tile floor was too cool to resist, so I pulled off my hot boots and socks before sitting down on it, stretching my bare legs before me. Painted in pale avocado, and furnished with rosewood settees, with matching chairs grouped around the room, I dreamed the room to be the exotic palace of an Indian prince.

Tired from all my exploring, I crawled under one of the cane bottom settees, took off my cowboy shirt, and laid flat on my back. I fell asleep with the naked boy from the picture in Abuelita's house dancing in my dreams.

SWEET DELIGHTS

The evening meal had barely ended when I stepped out onto the yard, away from the men discussing politics and the women gossiping about people I did know not care about. I could hear Papá leading the debate from his *taburete* as I strolled across the yard, the warm breath of summer on my face.

The hissing from *los faroles*, as the pressure was released and the kerosene mist burned through the gauzy hood, had been a new discovery for me. I had marveled at how easily their glowing white light was able to light up the entire house. But as I continued to walk away, the fainter the hissing of the lantern and the voices of the adults became.

I laid back against the cool black earth and gazed at the skies above. Squinting, I lost count of the starts winking at me across the Milky Way. An orchestra of crickets tuning their violins and frogs trumpeting their horns serenaded me. I heard the ancient owl's silent flight as it searched for mice scurrying in the fields. My friend Ms. Moon glowed, and I felt her silver light cloaking me. From where did this beauty come? Who or what had created such a marvelous world?

I must have been there a while, because I heard concern in Tia Dulce's voice when she called for me: *"Martincito...quieres chocolate?"* Little Martin...do you want some hot chocolate?

Sitting on the kitchen table bench, with Father on my left and Papá on my right, I fidgeted with anticipation, watching Mamá slowly shave the chocolate brick with the same knife that two days later I would use to slice the mortadella hanging from the store's crossbeam.

I remember standing on the *taburete* I had dragged into the room, climbing on top of it and aiming the sharp blade of Mama's big knife at the hanging salty treat. I wanted one thick slice to put on my buttered bread.

Just as I pulled the knife back, she was there behind me, grabbing it out of my hand. That was the first time I saw panic in her eyes, and it frightened me.

However, on that blessed night when Mamá handed me a mug of her special hot chocolate, the steaming scent of vanilla and cinnamon kept wafting under my nose. Fast as a lizard's tongue snapping at a fly, I closed my eyes and dove my tongue into the foamy treat.

I was delighted when I opened my eyes to see everyone watching me, their smiles genuine and wide. Surrounded by my family that night, I was as important to them as my friend Ms. Moon was to the night, the stars, and the endless skies above. There, at the center of my own universe, I was safe. I was loved.

FEAST

As the squealing pig fought in a spastic dance, Papá held him down and Father shoved the short-pointed knife into his heart. Then it was all over, and all its struggles turned flaccid at once. Papá and the other men congratulated Father for the proficiency he had so proudly shown, but I found no joy in such a task.

I understood about an animal's death. I had seen the workers at the store cut the chicken's throats and place them head down into a funnel to let the blood run. However, this was different, for Father had taken me over to meet the little black pig the previous afternoon, and he seemed friendly and smart, grunting with joy whenever I reached out and rubbed his head and his side.

I didn't see then the benevolence in Father's hand. I didn't understand the importance of his singular act. My soul didn't see what my eyes saw when he repeatedly felt the animal's chest until certain that he had found the precise location of its heart. I didn't stay around to witness the shaving and dismantling of all its parts.

It was late morning before I returned to the *lechón* roasting on the pit, lured by the smell of the citrus, spices, herbs, and the taste of smoke from the fat dripping on the coals. Somewhere in my tutelage, someone must have taught me to ignore the brutal beginnings of a feast. Perhaps some inherited instinct made me not remember the cuddly pig when I bit into its juicy roasted flesh.

My bewilderment over Father's calculated action to kill the pig melted when he brought me a fresh ear of corn to roast with his. Once blackened and roasted, we washed the ash away with fresh well water and salted them before gobbling it all down. My cousin Nicolás, who was four at the time, arrived on horseback with his parents, Consuelo and Ramón, in the early afternoon. Spotting him, I ran over to share my previous day's adventures. I pointed out the beauty of the zinnia forest to him, but he could not see what I saw. Too young to understand the poetry in nature I worshiped, or appreciate the polished cool tiles, he quickly bored of me.

Alone again, I joined the women in the kitchen. I had learned many a wise lesson from the stories they told. Like bees in a busy hive, every woman performed their duty until the table was set, smoothing the floral table clothes over four tables that had been placed end to end in the great hall. With the men already sitting at the table, the women brought overflowing plates of *lechón* and a bounty of food to them. *Congris*, *yucca* with rings of onions and chunks of garlic had been browned in a pungent *mojo* sauce. There were *tamales*, sliced red and green *tomates*, and *aguacates* sprinkled with vinegar, olive oil, pepper and salt. There was also fluffy crusted bread to soak up the juices, and crunchy *galletas*, which I used to scoop up the food rather than using my fork.

Depression glass pitchers had been filled with clear well water, sweetened with pineapple rind that floated with the ice cubes on top. There was sweet bubbly cider known as *cidra*, and red Rioja wine.

Curious, I reached for Father's wine glass, and he held it to my mouth. My first sip was tart yet velvety warming and tasted of cherries, strawberries, chocolate, and cinnamon all at once.

Nicolás and I argued over which one of us would devour the greatest number of tender ribs, and who would get the largest crunchy pig's tail treat.

All seemed right with the world that afternoon on the farm. The men talked and laughed as the women bustled to serve them before sitting at the table themselves. All was relaxed, happy, and I was full of hope and joy. We were family.

PRELUDE

There was something magical about that early morning at the farm. The scents from the damp earth, blooming flowers, ripening fruits, and wet grass floated on the cool mist that greeted me when I stepped outside made me feel as if I wasn't awake, but dreaming a perfect dream.

Stirred by my sudden appearance, the free-roaming chickens flew off the branches they had chosen for the night, surrounding me as I stood in the yard, eager for their daily dose of ground corn. The cow by the paddock's gate raised her head and stared at me with her big, watery eyes, relieved from having been milked. The scent and the sound of Father cranking the handle of the coffee mill called me back to the kitchen, where two slices of bread were roasting on the open flames for me. My mouth watered when Mamá sprinkled fragrant olive oil and salt on top and slid the plate before me.

Having vented the boiling milk to a frothy foam and cooled it to butter, as she had every morning, I was just in time to spread a thick dollop of it on my bread. I gobbled up my breakfast, excited to start. On that day, Father saddled up his old horse for us to visit everyone on the farm.

Reluctant at first, the tall creature lumbered out of the yard and down the path by the towering Linden tree at the back of the house. Soon, the horse broke into a trot, bouncing us up and down in the saddle.

At each of Mother's relative's houses, we stopped for water or coffee. I was surprised how at ease Father was with the families, and how welcomed we were in their homes.

By the time we reached the *arroyo* at the end of the farm, the sun was at our backs. When Father led the horse to water to drink, I ran after them, stumbling on a slippery rock at the stream's edge and banging my knee in the process. Without reproach, Father washed the wound and tied his crisp white handkerchief around it.

By the time we arrived home, the throbbing had ceased and I had forgotten about my scraped knee. Mamá and Tía Dulce took one look at my wrapped knee and laughed nervously. Tía grabbed Mamá by the arm, and together they fled to the safety of the pantry the second they saw Mother come in.

One look at me was all it took for her to scream and burst into tears. "*¡Pero Dios mio! ¿Qué es eso? ¿Qué le pasó?*" Dear God! What is this? What happened to him?

Fearful of her sister's mood, Tía Dulce shuffled me out the door and down the path to Papá's brother's house.

I screamed when my great aunt poured iodine on my knee and sighed when she wrapped it in clean gauze. The ordeal over, I sat on the floor, with their enormous white cat meowing and rubbing against my back as I enjoyed the sticky sweet slice of guava paste and salty white cheese that she had rewarded me with for being such a brave boy.

The house was unusually quiet upon our return. Evidently, Mother had locked herself in a bedroom, and Father was nowhere to be found.

Everyone looked the other way or ignored me completely when I asked where Father had gone. Too fearful of Mother's wrath to ask her, I wandered out of the house and down the path to where I had spotted the hummingbird the previous day.

However, it was late and the petals of the flowers were limp from the beating heat of the day, and there was no hummingbird in sight. So I picked up a discarded branch spearing a tuft of weeds, sat on the dusty ground, and scratched out the shape of the hummingbird with my stick.

CONFUSION

By the time Mother and I returned home from the farm in late August of 1960, the scab on my knee had popped off. It was then that she, without explanation, informed this six-year-old that Father would no longer be living with us. She left me alone to reason through the uncertainty.

Everything had been fine until the day of my accident. So I figured it had been my fault that Father left us. It was because of me that they quarreled when we were home in Havana, and now I was to blame for whatever happened on the farm.

Mother didn't seem sad or upset. She didn't shed a tear that I noticed. Instead, she appeared to be celebrating. Joyously, she sang her favorite songs as she hosed down her bedroom's dusty blue walls, scrubbing them with a broom and strong disinfectant soap before painting them in a shocking shade of blue as loud as the tail of a prancing peacock. *"¡Despojando el spirito de su amante!"* Washing away the soul of his lover from the house, I heard Mother cry. I didn't understand what a lover was, or why it was so important to wash her spirit away.

As time passed, Father would occasionally arrive in the evening and stay the night, but most of the time he stayed away. When I told Mother that I was confused, she didn't explain why he was sometimes home and sometimes not. I continued asking until, in frustration, she told me that he was working at his new *pollería* on the other side of town, and that it was easier for him to stay there rather than at home with us. This was new to me. No one had mentioned that Father had bought or worked at another *pollería*. Was it true?

My instinct was keen. I didn't believe her, but kept my doubts to myself.

His absence did ease the tension. Since I had prayed for us to have a peaceful life together, I figured this too was my fault. *"Es que ese vago me da mucho asco,"* I heard Mother say to Tía Cecilia one day. It's that this lazy bum repulses me.

"¿Si?" was all that Tía replied, with a nod.

When he did spend the night, Father and Mother slept in the same bed. He was noticeably affectionate with her, trying to kiss her good morning and goodbye before he left. However, she recoiled every time. I didn't understand. Was this a game? I had no one who could or would explain the situation to me.

Soon, the silence was shattered, and they returned to their bickering. The longer Father stayed away, the louder and harsher their fights became when he did return.

Living through all this constant change felt like a grotesque carnival ride where monsters and ghouls lurked in the shadows, determined to rip my heart out of my chest.

CODA

Epiphany Day 1962 brought great delight to me. Nearly eight, I was too old to believe in the three wise men anymore, but Mother seemed determined to let herself have one last innocent day—it wasn't hard to go along with the ruse.

That morning, I woke up to a big boy grasshopper-green bicycle and my first pair of shiny silver roller skates from Mother and Father, who had stayed home the previous night. Once I mastered my riding skills, not only did I impress him, but the neighborhood boys who had shunned me and chased me home every afternoon after school. They started hanging around outside our house, hoping I let them take a ride on my grasshopper-green bike. Concerned that I'd never see my bicycle again, I allowed them a ride with me, which they happily agreed to.

I could not wait to show Miguel as soon as he arrived for work. He grinned and teased me about the times three years earlier when he took me to the park to ride my first, much smaller bike. On one of those days, he removed the bike's training wheels, and I pulled away, pedaling so fast he could not catch up with me. I remember that day so well and the thrill I felt when the air rushed my face.

It had been a wonderful day—the day I happily shared my bike with my newly discovered friends. Blissfully, my mood was boosted during the few weeks before my birthday.

Mother surprised me with my first pair of long black dress pants, and Father presented me with a pair of brown loafers that I was to save for special occasions. Little did I know that Father had chosen my eighth birthday to officially move out of the house.

Once my party was over, he, without fanfare or a fight, walked out the front door, never to sleep under our roof again. Days passed without a word about when or where he had gone. As the weeks dragged on, I became afraid to broach the subject for fear I'd be blamed for his final departure.

Father's disappearing and reappearing, only to disappear again, left me dangling on the edge of guilt. Frustrated and worn out, a big part of me longed for a break from the constant upheaval. Back and forth. Back and forth. His disjointed pattern left me feeling unsafe and unsure about my feelings for him—I told myself that him finally being gone didn't matter at all.

One day in early spring, he showed up unannounced. Mother refused to let him into the house, so I sat with him on the front porch. His stoic face was drawn as he stared ahead at nothing. Leaning against the porch column, I watched the comings and goings of the neighbors, wishing to drown my thoughts in the noise of the crowd. The longer we sat there in silence, the lonelier I felt. Sadness engulfed us, and the curse of being unloved gripped me. We repeated this silent ritual every time he showed up unannounced.

One day, he insisted that Mother allow him to use the bathroom, but when he stayed in there for a ridiculously long time, she asked me to peep through the keyhole to see if he was okay. What was taking so long? Reluctantly, I knelt before the door and squinted through the keyhole. I froze, incapable of understanding exactly what Father was doing. He stood in front of the sink, the running water splashing against the tiled surround, stroking himself, slowly, deliberately. I didn't have a name for what he was doing, but it seemed a pleasurable thing. I could not move. I didn't want to move. I wished to learn.

I stayed there watching until Mother grabbed my arm and dragged me down the hall. Unrelenting in her quest for the truth, she continually questioned me about what I had seen. Standing over me, she insisted I tell her what I saw. There wasn't any chance of my escaping her wrath until I confessed. I exploded, "*¡Se está lavando el pito!*" He is washing his dick!

Her piercing glare, her face contorted in disgust, she eyed me like an evil god out for revenge. Then the tigress forced me out the door, telling me not to even think of coming back in until she called for me, and slammed the door in my face. I sat on the front porch, leaning against the sturdy column for what seemed like an eternity, stunned that no fight ensued. There was no yelling or screaming. No voices were raised. I saw and heard nothing. However, I jumped to my feet when the door banged open and Tío Patrício stepped out onto the porch. Tugging on Father's arm, he pushed him down into the sidewalk. Out of breath, he eased his grip on Father when he walked away, his head hung in shame.

Expressionless, he walked ahead without looking back at me. Down the block he walked, like a zombie, and disappeared around a corner.

Without explanation, Tío Patrício walked back into the house. The door stood ajar, but I didn't follow because Mother hadn't called for me. So I sat at the edge of the porch, staring at the sidewalk, wishing I had a stick with which to draw Father's face.

LONGING

To anyone who would listen, Mother declared that she was far happier without Father in the house. However, whenever she was alone, she walked around with a long face. In a heartbeat, she'd turn from deep sadness that made it difficult for her to get out of bed, to great agitation that had her pacing the floor. A caged beast at the Havana zoological park. She was stuck in the same cycle she was always spun in when Father left the house.

One afternoon, I was doing my homework when the volcano rumbling inside her erupted. Rushing past me, she bolted out of the house, just as she did the day of my birthday party when she dragged Father home from Benita's house, leaving me alone. I had no idea where she went, and she never explained when she returned hours later.

Shockingly, she started visiting the homes of women she had called *chusma*, demanding I accompany her. I had seen the hunger in their eyes as they waited in line for their chicken and egg rations. Of course, they were eager to welcome us into their house. Mother decided who got what and how much.

I was saddened to see them mock Mother behind her back, rolling their eyes in disgust, but I was as resentful as the women because she also controlled my life. They recognized anger in my eyes, patting my head or quickly kissing my cheek when Mother wasn't looking. We were the dying butterflies trapped in her spider's web.

She did anything and everything to make herself feel better. Feeling better for her was feeling superior to those around her. Needing something to brag about, she maneuvered her way into other's lives.

Hearing of an impending wedding, she'd dash out of the house to the bride's side, ready to charm her, with me dragging behind, insisting that I'd be the ideal ring bearer at their ceremony: *"Mira qué niño más lindo yo tengo. ¿Verdad?"* Look at what a beautiful boy I have. Do you not agree?

The women played the game, pretending to inspect the merchandise, me, but knowing all too well that Mother's request was an order to be obeyed. But she didn't stop there. *"Se parece a un angelito."* She sold me as the perfect angel, the innocent cherubim.

Within a few months, I had taken part in more weddings than I cared to recall. They were a blur—a nightmare of moments melted together into one long, painful memory. Mother could have cared less because she was to be the center of attention. Focusing her energy on the star of the day, herself, she'd make a new dress to put the others to shame. Then, off she'd fly to find new shoes and hat, succeeding despite all the rationing. She anticipated their adulation, and they delivered. Only then did she relax, her confidence restored.

Being a fidgety child, I hated standing completely still, holding some silly cushion for two rings I could never keep steady. My palms sweaty, I feared every second walking down the long aisle of the church, afraid I'd drop the shiny rings and have to chase after them as they rolled under a pew. I hated smiling for the photographer and the lewd wedding guests stuffing their mouths with cake and drinking too much. However, we stayed long after the happy couple left. The alcohol flowed as Mother danced the night away. Celebrating late into the night, we were always the last to leave.

At one of the weddings, a man whose presence I was unaware of, followed me into an empty room, where I hoped to hide from Mother and the partiers. Before I knew it, and without warning, he pushed my face into his crotch, the smell of which excited me. His action awoke something in me I hadn't been aware of—something I liked. After that, I became the one pushing Mother to make sure I was the ring boy for every neighborhood wedding.

After that day, I never cared about the procession, the photographs, or the cake. All I cared about was scoping the crowd in search of a man who was ready to follow me into a room—a man longing to press my face into his crotch. Their attention made me special, and I like being special because being the chosen one suppressed my angst. Like Mother, I thrived on attention. Back then, I wasn't aware that their actions were vulgar. It gave me pleasure. It satisfied that want clawing at me. I felt superior and I loved it. I never knew if it was habit or instinct that drove me to these men.

GAMES

We didn't go to the farm, but stayed in the city that summer after Father left. Disappointed, I tried to make friends with the boys on the block, but they never asked me to join in their games—I never could throw a ball in a straight line, or hit it once with a bat. Even when I pushed my way in, I felt lost because I didn't understand the rules of their games. So I convinced myself that, as Mother claimed, our money made us better than everyone one else. My insecurity, along with Mother's tutelage, had intensified my arrogance. I did not know that such cultivated conceit corrupts a child's psyche and ravages a wounded heart.

I became a bragger. Whenever one of the boys shunned me, I'd brag about all the things that we had that they didn't. I'm not certain why I did it, because it always ended with them beating me up. Still, I'll admit I enjoyed the thrill of their touch and them racing after me. After all, they were chasing me. I was the center of attention again.

After failing to connect with the boys and growing tired of being beaten up, I decided that I'd spend time with the three girls on our block. They'd gossip about things that, as a boy, I didn't know, and about boys they had crushes on. So I joined in, sharing my secrets about the boys I liked, even the men I thought were handsome and the feeling I got when I was with them.

Everything changed suddenly. They stood there gawking at me, their faces twisted and ugly. Then they'd pounce on me like the boys had and push me away. The sound of their laughter echoed down the block, and I walked home with my head down, certain that everyone in the neighborhood had heard them and agreed with their assessment of me. Desperate, I started visiting the neighbors I had visited with Mother. Since she was too occupied with her own interests, I did whatever I wished, going wherever I pleased. I even walked where she told me never to go. I hung around their houses until they invited me in. It was fun. I was starving for attention, and they showered me with praise.

I trusted the new people I met, as well as the adults I already knew, making myself available to anyone who opened their door to me. I trusted the overly friendly wives who handed me sweets, and their unshaven husbands who taught me how to flirt with them, telling me to bite my lower lip. I saw how cocking my head to the side and staring into their eyes made them grin and their tongue dart over their lips. I let them hug me close when they placed me on their laps. I marveled at how wide their nostrils opened, and I welcomed their quick burst of breath on my neck. I smiled when they told me I was a beautiful child no one could resist. I held tightly onto their necks until their rigid bodies fell limp and their heavy breathing stopped. But my anxiety never fully vanished because I wasn't certain I was doing the right thing. I was confused because, after it was over, they pushed me away.

ECLIPSE

The sidewalk's heat burned more than usual through my black orthopedic boots in the summer of 1962, when I was eight years old. This was just weeks after Tío Patrício had pushed Father onto the street. I hadn't heard from him since.

I began to wonder if Father was dead. What other thing could stop him from reaching out to me? I wasn't Mother. He didn't fight with me. Was he embarrassed after being discovered in front of the bathroom sink? Did he know that I spied on him? Was he angry with me?

That summer, we didn't journey to the farm. Mother refused to go, knowing that Papá expected her to explain what had been going on. I knew because I heard her say this to Tía Cecilia when she asked. "*¿Por qué ir al campo? ¿Para responder a todas las interrogaciones?*" Mother didn't want to be interrogated by anyone.

I lingered on my own with nothing to do. I walked down to the corner bodega daily, hoping that the men would not send me away. And there was always Fernando calling me over and offering me sweets.

It was an adventure. A treat. Getting free gooey pieces of candy from behind the bodega's display case. Chasing them down with a soda until my stomach ached.

The memory of that day is as fresh today as if had happened yesterday. It was lunchtime, and Fernando pulled the bodega metal doors down, as he always did. I was safe inside with my friend. I had no desire to go.

Fernando opens the half door to the counter and whispered for me to join him. I happily obeyed.

A fast embrace. A suffocating hug. *Aguardiente* kisses in my mouth. His tongue down my throat. My pants on the floor. Fernando forcing me onto his lap. A sharp pain. I gasped as he covered my mouth with his hand. My heart burst into flame. I felt nothing in the dark. Brown. Red. Sticky white running down my legs and into my pants.

DECONSTRUCTION

Stepping out into the summer heat, I looked around and up and down the streets. I was all alone. Everyone had gone home to take their nap. I stood alone on the outside of the bodega's metal doors, not knowing where to go. So I went home. Mother hadn't closed the store for lunch, and I walked unnoticed through the crowd of noisy shoppers and into the bathroom. I sat in the tub, not knowing what to do. I turned the shower on before I realized I was still wearing my clothes. Silently, I stood in the shower, careful not to breath too loudly.

The voices of the chatty shoppers rose and fell and rose again. Someone laughed. No one came in. The water rushed over me, and I pulled my shirt off and stepped out of my pants. My clothes sopping wet in the tub. I let the water rinse the brown and the red and the white away. I stood in the shower, shivering.

My teeth chattering, I stepped out of the tub, wrapped myself in a towel, and walked out, leaving my wet shoes and clothes in the tub, the water beating them clean. I dressed in fresh clothes. I took my crayons, pencils, and paper out of the drawer. I sat under the yellow Formica dinning dining table and began to draw. Red and purple and brown balloons, all framed with thick harsh lines that weighed them down as they tried to rise higher against a sky overpowered by shadows and clouds.

Mother passed by without stopping and said, "*¡Qué lindos!*" But I didn't reply. She was busy with her work, and

Father was no longer at home, and there was no one to talk to. And besides, no one wanted to hear my voice, small and dry. I never spoke a word of what happened that day to anyone. Only once. To a priest.

TRANSFIGURATION

The child who walked to his new school that fall wasn't me, but some other child I didn't recognize. I stood outside of myself to look at an unfamiliar creature in the mirror who had forgotten how to laugh.

My constant chattiness, my trusting willingness to engage with the world—nothing that I had been before was there. No one reached out to and hold me, and I reached for no one.

The child who walked into that fourth-grade class didn't know how to introduce himself or how to act. On that day, my ghost sat on the last row and didn't speak to anyone.

But there was a gift on that day waiting for me when my new teacher Rosita came by and sat next to me. She stayed behind and ate her lunch with me. And she placed her long thin hand on my head at the end of the day and spoke of the happiness she felt by having me in her class.

That somehow became enough for me—a new stranger in my life who possibly understood what I felt. A stranger I hoped would care for me.

RELIGION

The little poor people's church stood at the corner of a restful tree-lined street, a block further away from my school. A wide alley between it and the clergy house ran down its side and led to the auditorium where children and mothers were assembled, waiting for the proceedings to begin. Her nails polished and every hair of her head lacquered into place, Mother paraded me into the hall.

Two motherless butterscotch-colored boys with tight charcoal curls sat by themselves. Several rows away, seven girls and their mothers sat in a group. Looking at the girls, I laughed at their dresses, all oozing with eyelet and lace. The septet looked like a flock of pink Flamingos wading through a pond of meringue.

Being the first child in the family to attend catechism, receive First Communion, and become part of the church seemed particularly important to Mother, even if to no one else. I wanted to be a success. I wanted to be better than everyone else. I wanted to be noticed in the fancy shoes and pants that I had been given two years earlier on my eighth birthday, because I seldom had a chance to show them off. The shoes were so nice that I didn't tell anyone that my feet had grown a size too big. Instead, I bore the pain. They were worth it.

During my days as a ring bearer, I was being the ideal cherub and worrying about my performance to see beyond the layers of priestly gowns and carved statues atop the gilded altars. I never found God in those pantomimes. I didn't really know who or what God was.

Ever since Fernando hurt me in the bodega, I'd suffered an indescribable loneliness. A flash of guilt accompanied every stinging memory, and I hadn't the proper words to describe the sick feeling in my gut that haunted me. I was lost. I'd closed myself off from the world and no longer trusted the adults I once relied on. Still, I desperately wished to belong somewhere—anywhere—that was outside of the chaos inside my house, with Mother constantly painting the walls and pacing back and forth. Perhaps the God living inside this simple little church would welcome me into his house.

A short doughy priest and a towering nun—a ridiculous pair indeed—walked into the hall and a hushed ripple of nervous laughter trickled through the crowd. The priest's taupe tunic highlighted the redness in his face, and the nun, dressed from head to toe in black except for an overly starched wimple and equally stiff veil spreading wide from side to side, wore enormous black laced-up shoes. Her feet looked like those of clowns when compared to the old priest's childlike shoes.

I tried to listen. I tried to pay attention and learn the lessons they preached, but they were confusing and filled with nonsensical things that I knew nothing about. I wanted to believe what was being said, but no matter how hard I tried, their words spoken and the passages they read aloud didn't speak of the gentle, kind deity I wanted God to be. The more they spoke, the more bewildered I became over the perplexing of religion and the complexity of God.

I bated my eyelids to stay awake as they talked on, their speech obscured by my befuddled mind. Unable to hear what they were saying, I shot my hand in the air. The nun narrowed her eyes at me and nudged the priest, but before he had a chance to focus on me, I asked him who God was and why did I need to pray to the lifeless statues of angels and saints rather than talk directly to Him.

The hall fell silent, and everyone craned their neck to see what rude boy had interrupted God's earthly representatives. Glaring at me, Mother pinched my arm and whispered for me to shut up. I had asked the one question no one dared to ask.

Furiously, the nun barked at me, explaining that God was too busy to listen directly to my childish poppycock—*mis majaderías*. My face flushed with embarrassment when the priest pointed at me and rolled his eyes. A wave of laughter rippled through the crowd, crushing my vulnerable heart. My wish to belong dropped like a falling star into my lap. Singled out and ashamed, my wishes to be popular vanished in the roar of their laughter.

Sinking down into my seat, I tried to make myself small, but it was too late. Everyone had noticed. I was the center of attention, but not the way I wished—I wasn't in charge. So I stared down at my shiny brown shoes, avoiding the prying eyes burning a hole into my confidence. I sighed when the laughter ceased, and the nun and the priest continued their act for the Almighty.

A week later, I smiled broadly and approached the flock of Flamingo pink girls, but they stuck their noses in the air and pranced away. Unflappable, I moved across the room and sat down next to the butterscotch-colored boys. Surprisingly, they asked if I wanted to be their friend. At last, I'd found someone who accepted me as I was. They'd witnessed my humiliation and were still willing to welcome me into their group.

Much more knowledgeable than me about the church, I listened to their advice and did as they suggested: just play the game, even if my ten-year-old mind remained baffled by the Trinity, the Son, the Holy Ghost, the virgin birth, and the saints.

Having been born into the faith, they taught me the long prayers, and when to kneel, sit, or stand. The meaning of the rituals continued to illude me, but I played the game as instructed. That is, until the day I walked down the aisle to receive my first host. I looked around and all the other children appeared so humble before God as they approached the priest. So I concentrated as hard as I could, certain that the presence of God was nearby. He must have been, because everyone around me was so different. I was convinced that they were experiencing an ecstasy that eluded me. Was I too big a sinner for God to walk with? I prayed for him to whisper in my ear, let me know he was there with me? Guilt heavy on my head, I felt like a fraud.

However, when I saw one of the girls smirking at another after I accepted the host from the priest, the game was over for me. Attending mass and taking communion was simply one more task to cross off my list.

Something broke inside me. Still, I faithfully confessed my sins to the old red-faced priest whose breath reeked of coffee, tobacco, and rum, just as the domino-playing men at the bodega. I no sooner opened my mouth than he started to snore.

Where was God? So many people around the world worshiped him. They filled the pews of the churches and offered their hearts to him. Week after week, I searched for him, willing to give him another chance. On my knees, I prayed and offered my eager heart to him. I promised to do anything he asked if he would take away the unbearable loneliness dragging me under.

But when he didn't show his face to me, when he didn't save me from those who ridiculed me and tortured me, when he didn't bring Father home or make Mother look at me, I cursed him. I kicked and screamed and cursed him.

It was then, sitting alone in a darkened corner of the church, that he heard my cries. As abruptly as the storm outside had rushed through the streets, it suddenly stopped. Its winds halted and I heard the last raindrops pinged against the stained-glass window next to me.

Radiant with sunshine, like a rainbow, each jewel and facet shimmering in the bright light, God's light surrounded me. Across time and space, the light from my yellow kitchen kingdom had traveled to warm me once again.

I figured he had always been there, but I hadn't looked hard enough for him. He was there at the farm, alive in Mamá's zinnias when their faces smiled at me. There, in the flittering wings of the hummingbird's flight. There, when Abuela's kerosene lamp's lion flame chased the darkness away. Always there in her sweet rosewater scent.

TREACHERY

I was ten. What venial or mortal sin could I have committed in my life? What sins did I have to confess? Once in the confessional, I panicked and confessed to not obeying Mother's rules, and to answering back when she scolded me.

Week after week, I walked to church on Saturday mornings and stood in line to confess the same sins that I confessed to the previous week. The guilt about having nothing to confess was weighing me down. Should I have made things up? I figured God was listening and would know that I'd lied. That would be a sin to confess.

The euphoric swarm that swept through the church doors every Sunday, I reasoned, had been forgiven for some outrageous sins that they most likely had made up anyway. However, my sins were considered silly, brandishing me an outsider who didn't understand how things worked if you wanted to talk to God. I stood alone, communing with God through the sunlight.

I wanted to belong. I wanted to be overwhelmed by my confessable sins, pray for forgiveness, and join the mob in their delight.

I was a child—one amongst a crowd of very few boys, occasional men, overly dressed girls, and women busily cooling themselves with their fancy Spanish fans. Women who looked me up and down just as the domino-playing men always did.

Arching their brows, rolling their eyes, they'd whisper loud enough for me to hear: "*Es el loco ese que se sienta solo al sol.*" He is the crazy one who sits alone in the sun.

Young Padre Felipe arrived from the seminary that same year along with the endless summer rains. The moment I first saw him, I was possessed by him.

Tall, broad, but not fat, his black hair framed a polished white marble face that glowed under the altar's bright lights. Had it not been for his holy robes, he would have been described as *un señorito*—meaning, the son from a family with great wealth, influence, and class.

I changed my confession times to late Saturday afternoons so I could confess to him rather than to the old, red-faced priest, making sure that I was the last one in line— if we were alone, I was certain that I'd have the courage to speak of the secrets I'd never shared with a single soul. With the two of us, alone in God's house, I'd be safe.

He spoke in a caressing voice and assured me that he was my friend, and that I could share anything with him, even if I didn't think it was a sin. I rejoiced! I'd found one person that cared for me.

Willingly, I confessed about my crotch-smelling escapades and my rides in the neighborhood men's laps. I happily confessed to all the secrets in my life which I had never shared with anyone.

I never received a reprimand. Instead, he listened carefully to my stories and assured me that the things I spoke of were not really sins because the men only wanted to show how much they cared for me.

"*¿Y qué más?*" And what else? he gently asked. He coaxed the whole truth about my day with Fernando out of me. He gently nudged until I told him how Fernando pulled me onto his lap. I told him about the brown, the red, and the white that rushed down my legs and into my pants.

I felt nothing as I spoke, and in the emptiness that followed, in the stillness of the church, I heard nothing but the soft spit of candle flames burning in their stands. Though numb, I started to sob. The tears pooled in my eyes, overflowed, and ran down my reddening cheeks.

I couldn't breathe. I couldn't move. I couldn't speak to explain my tears. Frozen, I remained kneeling until Padre Felipe walked out of the confessional and tenderly lifted me to my feet, hugged me close to his warm body, and ran his fingers though my short crew cut. Suddenly, I could breathe. I was calm when he walked me out the side door, and across the wide alley to the small office at the back of the clergy house.

Pulling a chair close, he sat next to me. Leaning over me, he held my face in his soft manicured hands and kissed my forehead, my cheeks, my eyes, my lips. At that moment, that moment sparking with electricity, I knew that I'd do anything he asked. Taking my hand, he guided it to his lap.

Just then the old red-faced priest opened the door and peeked in. His sagging jowls, his sunken cheeks, his wrinkled flesh flushed red, then plum, then crimson before he retreated, banging the door shut behind him.

Hysterically, Padre Felipe jumped out his chair so fast, he knocked it over. Kicking the chair against the wall, he grabbed me by the scruff of my neck, drug me across the room, pushed me out the door, and slammed it shut. The sound of the lock clicking into place echoed down the alley. "*¡Apúrate, antes que el regrese!*" Hurry up, before he returns, he whispered harshly from the other side of the door.

Shaking, I stood in the alley, completely terrified that the old, red-faced priest would find me there. I looked left. I looked right. My thoughts spinning, I panicked. My knees pumping high, I ran as fast as I could out into the street. Blinded by the neon lights from the bar's sign across the way, I ran unable to see ahead of me. Our house was only six blocks away, but I couldn't find it. I was lost. I kept running, sweat pouring down the sides of my face. Nothing looked familiar. Nothing seemed the same as I raced down alleys and past strangers and past the bodega. The bodega. I knew where I was.

When I finally found my way home, I walked into an empty house. I looked for God, but he wasn't there in the dark. God could not survive in Mother's house, always shuttered against the light. We lived in the shadows—that place once called home that would never be a home again. That place where a boy lived with a mother and a father who gave him wonderful presents, cowboy shirts, roller skates, and bicycles.

I walked from room to room, turning on the lights before reaching my sleeping cot against the wall of the still dark vestibule. There had never been a light in my room except for an old lamp sitting on the floor.

No, I could not stay in my room. Hot, sweaty, and exhausted, I walked to Mother's brightly lit room, crawled under the covers, curled into a ball, and cried myself to sleep.

I stayed away from church for weeks, until Mother forced me to return, worried over what the neighbors would say. When I did return, it wasn't Padre Felipe's voice I heard behind the confessional. The recognizable scent of decay was evident, and I knew at once that it was the old, red-faced priest who was sitting on the other side of the wall. He didn't call my deed by its name, but his judging voice accused me of committing the unspeakable sin. That's when I knew he blamed me for tempting noble Padre Felipe to commit unimaginable deeds.

He didn't assign me hours of penitence prayers, but left me adrift, holding onto the massive guilt and remorse. He refused to grant me the absolution of the church.

I did kneel. I prayed my own prayers of penitence. I prayed for forgiveness, desperately wishing for a miracle. I worried that my actions hadn't gotten Padre Felipe into trouble. He loved me, didn't he? Like the men before him loved me, I wanted him to love me.

Not sure of what I should do, I sat by my favorite window, praying for a sign from God. Surely, he had forgiven me for my sin. I asked him to send me light. If the stained-glass window of Mary snuggling the Christ child to her bosom lit up, then I knew he had forgiven me, that he loved me, that he was on my side. However, when I heard the raindrops beating against the wedges of colored glass, I knew he wasn't coming.

Glancing up at Mary's face, shadowed by the column nearby, I was startled by the sternness of it and Baby Jesus's desperate expression as he tried to hold onto her, just as I'd tried to hold onto Mother.

God wasn't coming. God had abandoned me in my moment of need. The longer I sat there, the angrier I became.

If God did exist, he didn't exist for me. If God smiled, he wasn't smiling at me. Like all the others in my life, God was pushing me out into the street. I felt a tightness in my chest. I wanted to cry, but steeled myself, making a promise that I'd not let them see me cry again. Even God didn't deserve my tears.

Passing though the heavy wooden doors, I stepped out into the pouring rain and never returned to that church again.

It had been two years since my eighth birthday and the wonderful gifts from my parents. Two years since Father had left. Two years since men had enticed me to press my face to their crotches. Two years since I'd dreamed of love in the laps of the unshaven men I visited. Two years since I sat on Fernando's lap, only to be tossed away. Two years since I'd stopped playing games with those who rejected me. Two years of exile from everyone, and even myself.

The year I turned ten, I learned to be cautious. No longer did I trust the actions of those around me. In that year, my face tightened, and I lost my smile. I hardened. I became stern because not even God cared for me.

THE END OF HOPE

Mother and I were the last to arrive at *la finca* on that scorching sweltering summer day in 1965, when I was eleven years old. The branches of the mango trees in the yard hung low, perhaps from the weight of the ripened fruit, perhaps because they were too exhausted to push against the crushing walls of humidity. I had looked forward to seeing cousin Nicolás, but only Tía Consuelo had come. Once again, I was the only child at the house.

An enormous faded blue truck with tall wooden stockades running down the sides of its bed stood in the middle of yard. In and out of the house, the men loaded furniture and household necessities onto the truck.

Earlier that March, Mother and I had rushed to Abuela's house, and I sat by her side. I held her fragile hand, and she lovingly kissed my cheek. She died two days after we returned to the capital. I shocked myself when happiness filled my heart. She was in a better place. Though God was stern, I was certain he'd smile when he welcomed her to pass through the pearly gates. I sang cheerfully, knowing that she was now pain free.

This had been the greatest loss of my life so far, but I wasn't there to experience it for myself. It had been easy for me not to feel its pain. However, that August day at the farm, with the revolution in full swing and the government taking away the house and the farm that Papá and Mamá had labored to build, I could not run away from the pain. Beyond the imminent loss of my refuge, the only safe world I'd ever known, the entire family was changing forever. Repeatedly, the same questions echoed in my head: What would happen to us? What would happen to me?

Mother walked directly into the house as I lingered in the yard. When I finally went in, I had no other choice but to tightly lock my emotions because I didn't want to upset the family any more than they already were.

I was now eleven and no longer wanted to play. I'd drawn my last picture in the dirt with a stick, and gave up talking to the zinnias and my old friends, Ms. Moon and Mr. Sun. Still, I needed to play a happy child game for the adults. This had always been my job, after all. My child-like smile hid the turmoil inside me and lightened the mood of the heavy-hearted adults hauling their lives out the front door and onto a truck.

I needn't have worried because everyone was too busy to even ask how I felt about the loss. Aimlessly, I walked through the rapidly emptying rooms—the only acknowledgment of my presence being the constant demands for me to get out of the way. Then I no longer bothered to smile bravely for them because my strength was invisible to them. My heart cracking like a block of ice, I longed for a comforting touch, but no one noticed me.

By early afternoon, all the valuable contents had been loaded onto the truck, and everyone but Mother and Mamá came out to wave their goodbyes. In the driver's seat, Papá seemed anxious to go.

The family gathered in groups of twos and threes on the dry, fractured black earth they once called their own. Their dull smiles resting uneasy beneath their dead eyes, they painted a grotesque picture of Cuba's future for me. Without hugs, minus tender caresses, the atmosphere oppressing the once joyous family I remembered gathered around the table, laughing, joking, and enjoying a feast.

I wanted to reach out to Tía Dulce as she sat rigidly upright on the back of the truck, but she never looked my way, and with my heart caught in my throat, it was impossible for me to call her name. Her intense stare was affixed to Tía Nereida sitting next to her. So I recoiled and stepped back into the shade, no longer welcoming the bright light of day. Hope passed away on the farm that day, and with it the biggest piece of me.

In a last hopeless hurrah, Tía Nereida yelled to the crowd, joking that they were taking the contents of the house to make a great epic film. Briefly, the mood shifted, and a faint chorus of laughter washed over those gathered. Without fanfare, they silently waved goodbye as the truck drove away.

A deafening silence dropped on the farm. Even the chatty birds stopped singing as we watched the loaded truck drive past the great big tractor gates, cross over the railroad tracks, turn right onto the bumpy country road along the rail line, and disappear behind a dense cloud of dust.

Rooted to the ground, we stood frozen, watching the dust settle back onto the road. Like an uncontrollable nightmare, I couldn't rewind the scene and change the narrative. Life determined to play it out to an unedited finish that I had no power to control. Everyone stood still as if they expected the truck to return, but the horizon sat near barren, with nothing left to look at but the flat miles of harvested sugar cane fields that stretch far beyond the rail line.

I stood alone as everyone filed back into the house. I wanted to cry, to break the tightness gripping my chest. I tried to cry, but I shed not a single tear. I had cried my last tear a year earlier, when Padre Felipe pushed me out of his office and slammed the door in my face.

In the kitchen, I found Mamá trembling like a wet newborn bird in its nest. Wanting to comfort her, I wrapped my arms around her shoulders and leaned my head against hers. Immediately, she stiffened, her body rigid with rejection. I felt dead! Then I noticed Mother slumped against the wall, with a dour expression plastered on her face. Only then did I first see how much like each other the two women were.

Metamorphosis

P uberty was my birthday gift in 1966. Now twelve years old, I stood before the full-length mirror, staring at the quickly changing me. A shapeshifter, I carried both my parents with me. The roundness of my Mother's face was losing ground to Father's angled, handsome face. I ran my fingers over the peach fuzz on my chin and wondered who'd teach me how to shave. None of this had been explained to me, and I was too stubborn to ask for help. I'd have to somehow find out on my own.

Of course, this insecurity made me uneasy, and I'd lash out at anyone who made me the butt of their joke. I'd fly into a rage! My head was full of thoughts and doubts and unspoken secrets that spun like a tornado across the vacant acreage, the abandoned fields in my head. There were a few explanations that dropped into my lap.

I was enlightened by my sexual awakening and realized what Father had been up to when he locked himself in the bathroom and refused to come out. Recently, I'd learned the pleasure of my own company. What was once a sin was now a pleasure without which I couldn't live. It was a sensation like nothing else. I fully understood the pleasure that my rides had brought to the men whose laps I'd sat upon. But I no longer cared to sit on their laps. I wanted them to sit on my lap—I never again wanted to be their prey.

INCEPTION

O ur fence games had ended almost as soon as they had begun on the day Sebastián's aunt caught us when I was five. However, now that I had perspective, the memories of him tempting me from the other side of the fence began to play on my mind until they became a preoccupation for me. They haunted me from the time I got up to the time I went to bed. Whenever I used my own hand to satisfy myself, I thought of him and his hand down his pants. Soon, I was calling his name whenever his aunt left the house. Finally, our game resumed.

This time, I didn't pull my hand away. Instead, I ran it across his crotch. Reaching through wire, he rubbed my crotch but nervously kept an eye out for his aunt. Everything was different on that hot July afternoon in 1966, because that summer, we were no longer innocent. Sebastián was no longer a boy of fourteen, but a man of twenty-one. I was a grown boy, now twelve.

Sebastián was easy to seduce, easy to lure into the house. I'd stare into his dazzling hazel eyes, as I had perfected with the unshaven men. I told him that I'd leave the back door open because the house way too hot. *"Dejo la puerta abierta porque hay mucho calor."* We knew that Mother nor *los tíos* ever stayed home on Sunday afternoons. He knew—everyone up and down the block knew—that I was left alone in the house. I'd flirt with him and dare him to cross the line, until one day he agreed to come in.

In anticipation, I frantically ran from room to room, closing all the windows and securing the shutters to make certain that no one could see or hear anything.

I stood against the kitchen counter in anxious anticipation, completely blind as to what was about to take place, my head throbbing with my erection's every pulse. Minutes dragged on like hours as I waited for his shadow across the floor. Except for the sound of my heart beating, it was dead silent in the heat.

For years, I'd kept away whenever I saw him tinkering in his yard. But now, I welcomed him. It was evident how much his body had changed from the skinny boy he once was. Every muscle in his chest was perfectly formed. The faint rust-colored hair that ran from his stomach into his boxer shorts had grown into copious thick curls.

My entire body shook when he appeared before me. We didn't embrace. His arms hanging limply by his sides, he rested his head against my chest. All was still. When our heartbeats skipped in unison, he gently pressed his lips to mine. We embraced, and our kiss flipped from a gentle touch to passion, our tongues diving and twisting in one another's mouth. Suddenly, our tongues were everywhere. Our chests. Our thighs. Our calves.

Kneeling before me, he licked my belly button, unzipped my pants, and slid them down to my ankles. His mouth was warm and inviting. I gasped when he took me in.

Aggressively, he carried my naked body into the inner sanctum of the house. I whispered an emphatic *no* when he headed for Mother's bed, and shook my head when paused outside *los tíos*' bedroom. I pointed to my unmade cot, and he laid me down as if I were a newborn baby. In a feverish whirlwind of kisses, licks, and bites, he moved up and down my body before he sat on top of me. Up and down, he bobbed as I instinctively thrust inside him. Time stood still. Minutes whizzed by like seconds, and seconds raced on one sweaty moment at a time.

Suddenly, his entire body tensed, the veins popped out on his neck and his muscles pulsed. Quivering, he starred into my eyes, his quick, deep inhalations burst into a pant before he finally gasped.

Exhausted, Sebastián rolled off me and stretched out beside me, resting his head on my chest. He wrapped his arms and legs tightly around me. Then, trembling, he cried. We lay there a little while until his sniffles ceased.

Then, without explanation, he hopped out of the cot, hurriedly pulled his boxers on, and ran through the house and out the back door. Naked, I stumbled to the doorway, where I had waited in anticipation of him to appear. The longer I remained there, the more frightened I became. I didn't understand. What was I to do next? Why was he so passionate and happy until our game had ended? What did I do wrong? What would I say when next I saw him? I wanted to hold him, let him rest his head against my chest, show him affection, but that wasn't to be.

The next time we did see one another, he was cold, refusing to look me in the eye. I responded with the same coldness.

However, in the dark hours of early morning and late night, my anger for him turned to self-loathing. Rejected. Abandoned. He'd run away as Father had. I'd failed him in some way, but I couldn't figure out how. I didn't know what imperfection of mine kept sending away the people I loved.

CRUELTY

Miguel continued to work at the store despite there being nothing to sell for many days at a time. So Mother decide to close the doors on the afternoons we didn't have any chickens and eggs. She told him to go home when she closed early but he always stayed until the end of his workday.

Having him manage the store had brought new freedoms for her, which she seemed eager to explore. Even though I was now twelve, Miguel had continued to take care of me. Mother irritated me when she'd disappear for days at a time. Without a word as to where she was going and with whom she was traveling, she'd pack her best shoes, finest clothes, makeup, and of course her fancy high-heeled slippers and nightgown, into her lacquered overnight case. Then, joyfully, off she'd dash.

When she did eventually return, she offered no explanation as to where she had been. *Los tíos* simply looked at her and walked away. My inquiring about her adventures only led to argument, and I was determined not to fall into the same pattern Father had gotten trapped in. So I convinced myself that it didn't matter. But it did.

Deep down, I understood her desire to be with someone, to find someone to love her, to find someone she could love. Even so, I could not allow my sympathy for her to soften my anger. It was easier to live in a state of anger because being angry dulled the pain. I walked with disappointment and hurt.

Why couldn't she stay the loving mother she'd been that time when I was ill with the flu? She sat with me around the clock, mopping my brow, feeding her chicken soup to me, holding the spoon to my mouth. She'd fluffed my pillow and brought me Coca-Cola and forced me to drink buckets of water. Obediently, I did everything she said because I loved her as the devoted mother. I thought something had changed in her, and that she would remain the mother I'd forever wished her to be. But she only stayed for the duration of my illness. I even pretended to be sicker long after I'd recovered. However, there was no fooling Mother. She saw through my charade and swiftly shed her mother act to continue her pursuit of happiness.

Most days, I came home to an empty house after school. Mother had surprised me with ring of keys of my very own. So, I let myself in. Even if Miguel were in the store, I took care of myself, eating whatever I could find. On the days when there was no ready food available to me, I didn't eat until Tía Cecilia got home and cooked a meal. Often, we were forced to see what Tío Patrício brought home. If there was nothing left to eat, we illegally raided the store for eggs.

Those were the only hours when life felt normal to me. Once the meal was over and the dishes had been cleaned, *los tíos* returned to their room to be together, and I was left alone in our empty rooms.

One afternoon, as I approached the house, I noticed that the shutters and the door were locked tight. I was stunned to find Miguel behind the counter, stroking himself as Father had done at the bathroom sink.

Standing at the edge of the counter a few steps away, I stared at his big hand moving back and forth. Intently, I watched as he slowly stroked himself. His enlarged dark pupils reduced the glowing ring of white that framed them. He gestured for me to step forward. Hesitant for but a moment, I eagerly took over for him. I had dreamed of that moment so many times that it felt natural for me to comply.

What started as a onetime seduction, rapidly turned into a regular occurrence, as his closing the store early became more frequent. Hoping for a rendezvous with him, I'd race home from school. Enthralled with Miguel and his game, the pain of Sebastián's rejection faded. I rarely saw him in his yard, but one day when I did, I bragged about the things Miguel and I did until his hazel eyes filled with tears and he started to weep. I told myself that I didn't care, and started to walk away, but turned at the last moment to point to the open kitchen door.

Uncertain as to what might happen, or even what I wished would happen, I was excited when Sebastián took the bait. Wearing nothing but his boxer shorts, he walked over to Miguel and me, attempting to join us in our dance, but Miguel blocked him with his arm to prevent him from touching me. He remained there, listening to our labored breathing, our moans and gasping for air. Then, lowering his head, he quietly exited the same way he came in.

Even though I hadn't touched him, I was glad that Sebastián followed me into the house. Having shared the experience with two people I cared about more than anyone else in the world, I felt loved.

SCANDAL

A chill ran down my spine when I saw a herd of women barreling toward the house, running behind an ambulance, its sirens screeching. A hungry look in their eyes, they dodged traffic and circled the ambulance that stopped in front of our house.

Two men dressed in white jumped out and banged on the door of Sebastián's house, rushing in the moment his aunt opened the door. Within minutes, the crowd expanded down the sidewalk as the domino-playing men from the bodega had joined the gossiping mob. From our front porch, I strained for better view over the heads of the flock as the men in white carried a quivering Sebastián. Despite the handkerchief that partially covered the lower part of his face, the large crimson stain that ringed his lips and ran down his neck was apparent.

"*¡Mira! ¡Mira! ¡Mira! ¡Se envenenó! Dios mío, eso es mercurocromo.*" Look! Look! Look! He poisoned himself! Dear God, I heard a woman cry, pointing out that it was Mercurochrome.

A wave of comments rolled through the crowd as Sebastián's knees buckled under him, and he had to be held up by the two men, who hoisted him by the shoulder, and his aunt stretched her arms out to block the mob from coming near. Once he was safely in, the ambulance pulled away from the curb, its siren spinning wildly.

Alone, at the edge of my porch, I watched the mumbling crowd disperse. Clutching my knees to my chest, I locked my arms around them and rocked back and forth. My insides vibrating, I stared at Sebastián's aunt's house. It was dark before I ventured back in.

I didn't turn a single light on as I walked to the vestibule and reached my cot. I sat staring at my beautiful headboard that was never set up because I hadn't a bedroom of my own. I searched the silence for something, a single sound, anything I could pretend was noise alerting me that an adult had entered the house, that someone was coming to check to see if I were all right. But nothing was right, and I didn't know how to make things better. What was the answer to the question I didn't know how to ask?

Stretching out on my cot, I turned to face the wall and covered my eyes with my hand.

More than two months passed before another ambulance, its sirens still, stopped at Sebastián's front door. As the two men in white helped Sebastián to the door, he gazed around as if he'd never seen the place before. When he spotted me, his face was void of emotion as if I was a stranger. He no longer knew me. I had been erased. Until Mother explained exactly what had happened, I couldn't comprehend what he'd been through: "*Ay pobrecito, le dieron electroshock. Pero no entiendo porque está muy bobo.*" They'd given him electroshock, but Mother didn't understand why this had made him so dumb.

Sebastián never recovered. He no longer recognized me, and never gazed at me with his dazzling hazel eyes, because they were now dull. Never did he speak to me or anyone else again. His heart-wrenching silence intensified my guilt. I felt responsible for what he'd done to himself. After all, I was the evil one who had tempted him. The one who had enticed him to walk through the kitchen door. The one who had offered him an encounter with Miguel and me. His lifeless eyes were a reminder of what I'd done, and my guilt grew stronger with each passing day.

DESERTION

As soon as Sebastián returned home in late September, Miguel stopped working at the store. When I asked, Mother said that the government had decided to close it. Miguel simply left one day without as much as a goodbye. One day he was there, and the next day he was gone.

His change had been abrupt, from the moment that Sebastián had been taken away, by turning into someone distant and cold who never again kept the door closed or waited for me to come home.

When I'd arrive home, he'd step out onto the porch and wouldn't step back in unless there was a customer stopping by for their weakly ration of eggs. By then, no one had seen a chicken for months. At the end of his day, he simply locked the front door and didn't look back.

And so, I was left alone in the house every afternoon and every Sunday, with nothing to do but sit on the porch or stare at the people with somewhere to go and the traffic passing by. I sat there and watched until nightfall.

What else could I have done? I'd long angered the neighborhood boys with my insecure boastings about being better than them. I'd made the girls squirm with my talk of boys and men.

Desperately lonely, I broke the promise I'd made to myself to never again be the prey. I returned to the house of the men who desired me, and even to Fernando's empty bodega. But instead of being warmly greeted, I was shunned. Now, nearly a man, I was no longer the boy they craved. I was met with disdain. Their shame present in the young man before them, they looked me up and down with disgust.

My quest for love ended with more self-loathing, regret, and guilt. My mind reeled from their rejection, and somehow I needed to find a way to move on.

CAROUSEL

Round, squat, short-limbed, and sad, Valentín looked like the cartoon frog I watched on our grainy black and white TV. But just as in the cartoon, everyone forgot about his looks the second he opened his mouth and started to sing in a soulful Baritone, which brought joy to one's soul and tears to one's eyes.

When he sang, his bulging blue eyes sparkled like sapphires in the light. His wide nose and thick lips which had earned him the *Bembón* moniker always used to describe a man with a questionable birthright, became a sensual asset.

Whenever some of the neighborhood women raised their brows while asking: *"¿Y su abuela dónde está?"* to inquire where he was hiding his black grandmother, Margarita, my mother, would shun their disparaging insinuations about her new boyfriend. In defense of him, she pointed out the pinkness of his doughy skin and his thick mane of tight corn-colored curls.

Valentín appeared in our lives in time for Christmas in 1966, when I was twelve—a few months after Miguel had left. I walked into the dining room, and there he was, sitting at the head of the table as Mother served him lunch, smothering him with kisses and hugs.

By this time, I'd gotten used to Mother's parade of boyfriends and admirers, which made the neighbors' tongues wag in delight—referring to her as the neighborhood prostitute. Despite the obvious disappearing for days at a time, with her nightgown stuffed into her overnight case, she proudly proclaimed herself a pure and honest woman, and that her virginity had returned: *"¡Mira, que mi virginidad ya regresó!"*

Whenever Valentín was in the house, Mother was happier than I'd ever seen her, and I found myself at last able to breathe. I was grateful to him and thankful that her dark mood had disappeared. Now joyous, her repartee was humorous—a sight I'd never beheld before. Ever cautious Tía Cecilia was bold enough to boast that Mother had morphed into the eighteen-year-old young woman all her sisters had once cherished.

Mother, relaxed and cheerful, looked younger than her thirty-eight years. Coyly, a mischievous smile on her face, she spurned the comments about her being much older than her thirty-one-year-old boyfriend, to whom she never admitted her age.

Relieved that the tension in the house had subsided, I was quite willing to go along with her virginity farce or anything that she said. Even If I was supposed to be the man of the house, I presented no obstacles to Valentín sitting at the head of the table. Although she never once asked if his presence was fine with me, I didn't care because life was certainly better whenever he was in the house. On the flip side, and though I defended her to the neighbors, I was ashamed of her blatant lies and living in sin. Most of all, I resented her for making me feel that I was in her way, and detested the times she'd pompously declared that she was living her life for herself and not for anyone else. *"Ahora viviré mi vida para mí."* I despised her battle cry.

Oh, but Valentín had such gifts! And he treated me like the grown-up I pretended to be. Never ordering me about, he listened to and respected what I had to say. Despite his sparkling sapphire eyes, he was a safe match because I wasn't the least bit attracted to him, and he certainly wasn't into boys.

He treated us kindly and gave us a magical life that we had heard about, but believed we'd never see. Even though we had lived a comfortable life for a time, we were, after all, peasants.

Besides, there was little to brag about in our section of the city. We'd moved from a respectable neighborhood with beautiful houses, where our dentist lived across the street, to a ratty area so Mother could buy her own *pollería*—a place where the hen ruled the roost, and Father was just an employee? What was it all for, anyway? The revolution had ended that dream. Like everyone else, our rations never quite filled our bellies, and with each year that progressed, the neighborhood's buildings were more neglected. We lived in squalor and filth.

However, with Valentín in our lives, none of that matter. So we ignored the sordidness that engulfed Havana, and concentrated on fulfilling our dreams, which were so close we could taste the good times ahead. Stepping into his world of cabaret shows at the important nightclubs that catered to the affluent foreign class, mostly Russian or Czech, was entering into a fairytale I prayed would rescue us from the ills of our past.

Beautiful men populated this new world. At each table, in every direction I looked, the Russians and Czechoslovakians sat. I was transfixed on those strikingly handsome creatures, and marveled at their translucent skin, golden hair, fair eyes, their deep throated, honey-tongued voices, and confident, animated gestures. Like ghosts, they appeared before me when the cloud of smoke from their sweet-smelling cigarettes dispersed. Dressed in our best, off we'd go to dine at the fine restaurants only available to the few allowed to enter through their doors.

There were nights at the opera and the theater to be moved by *la Verbena de la Paloma* or one *zarzuela* after the other. But for me, the most treasured evenings were our nights at the ballet. Watching those beautiful gods dancing to *Giselle*, *Coppélia*, and *Swan Lake* sent my soul soaring into outer space, and I dreamed of joining them.

Secretly, I dreamed of escaping to the glory of the stage, but I never brought it up because it was considered unmanly and queer to my family. I figured if they forbid me taking piano lessons when I was nine—a feminine pursuit in their miniscule minds—I knew my dancing would be viewed as a great mistake. Mother insisted that I play the guitar, an instrument worthy of a boy's time. I refused.

Valentín introduced us to the finer things in life. Not only did he spoil Mother with lavish gifts, but me as well. He brought me—from where, I had no idea—tailored suits, modern clothes that no one else had, and hand-crafted European shoes. Like a responsible parent, he taught me the proper way to sit at the table, what utensil to use, and which wine I should be drinking with what course. I listened intently when he taught me the art of sitting still, of being quiet, and the importance of paying attention when others spoke, reminding me that I should speak once I'd been acknowledged, and only when asked to comment on subjects that I had knowledge of—how to be a gentleman, seemingly educated and refined.

In our naivety, Mother and I both believed that we'd transformed ourselves into people of importance. Reveling in our childish pride, we'd convinced ourselves that we could fool anyone with our charm and polished good looks. We'd conquered a new frontier and were anxious to move on.

REUNIONS

Father's phone message on Epiphany Day of 1967, just weeks before my thirteenth birthday, was brief. At least, that's what Mother said, without emotion, telling me that he planned to pick me up that Sunday at ten.

I only felt excitement as I sat on the porch, where I'd watched him walk away the day he stood at the sink.

I should have been angry at his abandonment, but I wasn't. The wheelbarrow full of questions and demands which I had long planned to dump at his feet, had magically emptied itself when I was told of his call. Thanks to Valentín's gifts, I eagerly dressed in my British rock star ankle boots with their slanted heels and pointed toes, my narrow pants, and fitted long-sleeve striped shirt.

Almost five years had passed, and I feared he would not know who I was because, at five-foot-seven, I had grown taller than him. Plus, having inherited Mamá's long arms, and with my one-hundred-twenty-pound frame, I seemed taller still.

He was late, and distracted by my own paranoia, I hadn't noticed the pale mint and turquoise Oldsmobile that stopped in front of the house. For years, I'd begged Father to buy a car, even insisted that it could only be an Edsel because I liked its horse-collar grille. I was thrilled thinking that the car was his gift of atonement to me.

Inside the car, a round-faced young woman with Andalusian skin and shoulder-length black waves sat next to him. Who was this woman?

When Father hugged me, I felt as if no years had passed. He couldn't believe how much I had grown: *"¡Pero hijo! Mira que alto tu estás.* The essence of his voice reminded me of Abuela's *guajira* chant. The moment seemed complete, as if she had orchestrated the reunion from her grave.

Once inside the car, Father introduced Zoraida as Alejandro's sister, and therefore Cousin Sandra's aunt. She whispered, *"Mucho gusto,"* and lowered her eyes.

I instantly knew that Abuela had granted three wishes: a reconciliation with Father, the hope of a calm family life, and reconciliation with Benita.

Father, Zoraida, and I walked down the same alley that Father, Mother, Tía Cecilia, and I had walked on our arrival to the capital that day, with the orange and purple sky above our heads. At the end of the path, the familiar group of men sat playing dominoes. And just as she had always done, Benita ran to welcome us back. It felt as though only days rather than years had elapsed.

Shortly after lunch, Benita took the three of us across the street to Sandra's house. We passed my old school and our old apartment. Exuberant, I ran ahead and knocked on the door. I gasped when a strikingly beautiful young woman opened the door. Interestingly, Sandra's light-brown curls were just like Celestino's. I'd never noticed that her eyes were the same moss color, and that she was as gregarious as he. Even though I'd been in their tiny apartment many times, somehow it looked so different. Everyone was jolly, and I was ecstatic to be with the people I loved. It had never occurred to me that I could have taken the bus on my own to visit them. Had I inherited Father's ability to easily walk away and forget? I shook the thought from my head. I refused to follow in his footsteps.

Instead, I wished to remember the happy days of eating breakfast with Sandra at our special table, and the hours spent coloring and drawing with our crayons.

Soon, I'd be celebrating Father's wedding day. Soon, I'd spend calm Sunday lunches at his and Zoraida's house—a comfortable place filled with tranquil days of hope as we waited for another new soul to be born. I dreamed of a promising time ahead as we all gathered around my brother Tomás's crib. I loved him from the moment I first saw him. He was never a stranger. He was so familiar that I was convinced we'd met in a previous lifetime.

Graciously, we ignored the fact that my new brother had been born just three months after Father and Zoraida's wedding day.

ACCEPTANCE

Father and I sat on the front seat of the massive Oldsmobile. Zoraida sat with Tomás in the back. On that cool November morning of 1967, there were no clouds in the sky as we traveled past the familiar ocean and green countryside I once waved at as a boy. We were almost there. A quick right, a left, and across the little town, we rolled to a stop at the familiar lime-colored house at the end of the last block. No one had lived in the house since Abuela's death. We parked the Oldsmobile there and walked to the blue and white railroad depot to board the same *guaguita* that had taken us to *la finca* in 1961, when I was six.

We were on our way to Abuela and El Viejo's old farm, which had been turned over to Uncle Nenico not long after I was born. This time, we didn't take the *guaguita* to the end of the line. We got off at the sugar mill and started to walk down a narrow path.

Unknown cousins and relatives waved from the fields as we walked toward the end of the lane. Father explained that I was part of a large family clan which Mother had never allowed me to meet. I didn't understand, but in the thrill of the moment, I didn't care to reason why.

The rectangular whitewashed house with few windows and doors crouching below its low palm leaf roof seemed quite small. At the kitchen door, a tiny woman probably as old as Mamá stood by to welcome us. The sun highlighted the few blond strands adorning her white hair. I remember her eyes being a pale blue, but maybe they were gray.

Father introduced her as El Viejo's sister Juanita, who kept house for my Uncle Nenico during the day since he was busy running the farm. I couldn't imagine why I had been denied meeting such a sweet soul whose touch was as gentle as Abuela's.

In late afternoon, Father gave me a tour of the farm—no more than a plot of land with room for the house, a well, an outhouse, a pigpen, a paddock for their horses, oxen, and one cow. Chickens roamed in the petite yard, and a stone path ran around the side of the house that faced the setting sun, bathing everything a glowing haze. Running the length of the walkway, a mostly dormant garden stood. But in my mind, I saw it as it must have looked in late spring. I imagined marigolds and fragrant herbs lining the edges: *perejil, tomillo, romero, cebolla, cebollín, cilantro, ajo y aji*, all mixed in an explosive wave of color and scent. Not far away stretched a large planting of corn. Further still, cucumbers and beans climbed the fence at the end of the yard. Nearby, meandering pumpkin vines were enveloped in velvety orange blooms. In the distance lay the sugar cane fields whose abundance provided a reliable source of income.

With an impish grin on his face, Father looked around to make sure that no one could hear him, before telling me that Nenico was able to keep the farm because with it being so small, the revolution had no use for the land.

That evening, as Zoraida and Juanita cleaned up after dinner, Nenico, Antonio—Benita's brother who lived and worked on the farm—Father, and I sat around the kitchen table. We listened to my uncle lead the conversation, just as Papá had led the conversation at his house.

As I listened, a streak of anger pierced my heart because Mother had kept me away from my family. However, it soon faded as I dreamed of future visits to the newly discovered plot of earth and my paternal family who tamed it.

Trips to *la finca* had ended more than two years earlier when a group of autocratic government officials showed up at the house and demanded that Papá and Mamá turn over the keys to the tractor and the house, giving them an hour to pack. So they packed what they could easily carry away.

To add salt to the wound, one of Papá's nephews, the leader of the government pack, stood guard at the gate as Papá and Mamá began the mile walk to the nearest house. This was the biggest betrayal of all, for this man didn't only betray his uncle, but his entire family.

It didn't matter that all the valuables from *la finca* were safe at their house in town. Visiting them at their new place could never replace the farm for me. It had never been the beautiful furnishings that made *la finca* a haven for me. Rather, it was the sweet scent of the black earth and the climbing Jasmin where the finches happily sang and puffed up their chests. The magic of Mama's zinnia garden. The coolness of the polished tile floors. The freedom I felt while riding Father's stubborn white horse.

It must have been quite early because the roosters had just started to sing. I was awake and eager to explore the marvels of nature in the cool morning mist.

I wrapped myself with the same bright-colored quilt that used to lay at the foot of Abuela's bed. Quiet as a mouse, I tiptoed across the living room's dark tiled floor to the clay-floored gathering room. I paused at the kitchen's threshold when I saw Nenico sitting at the table. He was facing away from me. Antonio stood quite close to him. The enticing aroma of strong coffee and refried pork wafted under my nose.

Frozen, I watched Nenico reach behind and take Antonio's hand. I cupped my hand over my mouth when they kissed to cover my near gasp. I'd just witnessed honest affection between two men. This was love! At once I knew that I wanted what they had for myself someday.

TURBULENCE

I didn't know about Valentín's plans to leave Cuba for Spain. I didn't know that Mother had decided to follow him. She had never spoken to me about it.

The day after I returned from Nenico's farm, she informed me our lives were about to change. I was stunned by how easy it seemed for her to leave everything and everyone behind. Wouldn't she miss Papá, and even Mamá, despite the uncomfortable distance between them?

And what about me? What about my wishes and dreams? What about my new family with Father, Zoraida, and baby Tomás? What about my dreams for a life with Nenico and Antonio at their farm? After all, the farm was a part of my inheritance as well. I could've been happy there. I was sure of it. I could visit Nicolás's family farm, which was easily reachable on horseback. I would've like that—getting to know my cousin, at last. My imagination met no boundaries as I dreamt of what could be ahead on my path.

I rebelled. I told Mother that she was free to follow her man, calling him her *chulo*—her pimp—as some of the neighborhood women referred to him, knowing that this word pierced her pride. I wanted her to feel the wretched pain she had caused me. I informed her that I'd be leaving her and moving in with Father. I'd leave the city and move in with Nenico and Antonio at their farm. Her eyes blazing mad, she howled like a wounded beast.

Every word she uttered sliced through me. She stuck the knife in my heart and twisted the blade. She proclaimed that she'd been granted sole custody of me. Body and soul, 1 was hers. She made it crystal clear that I'd not be allowed to visit Nenico and Antonio ever again. "*¡Eso no es posible! ¡No puede ser! No lo puedo permitir.*" It is not possible! It can never be! 1 can't allow it. She cried with desperation in her eyes.

I ran out of the house and down the six blocks to the park where Miguel had once taught me to ride my bike. 1 dropped onto the bench by the waterless fountain, so enraged that 1 was shaking. 1 stared at the broken cement slabs beneath my feet. Frustrated, 1 gazed at the buildings and houses across the street. 1 shook my head. It was as if 1 was seeing the neglect around me for the first time, the patched up busted windows and the peeling paint, the crumbling stucco, and the rotting wooden balustrades. My head spun with questions that only 1 could answer. Was this where 1 wanted to be? What would become of me when 1 turned fifteen? Would 1 be drafted into the military? Would 1 be safe with Nenico and Antonio on the farm?

It was hot, and my stomach ached. My face was wet with sweat, and my head was spinning. 1 wanted to scream.

What was left for me in Cuba if 1 stayed? My days at *la finca* had ended on that hot August day in 1965, when the contents of the house had been packed on the back of the big blue truck and driven away. Besides, 1 hadn't actually received an invitation from Nenico and Antonio to return or visit them again. 1 began to ask myself why 1 should stay. Why shouldn't 1 follow Valentín? He treated me well and spoiled me with gifts fit for a son. He listened to me and respected what 1 had to say. He brought calm to our frantic household. Mother was bearable when he was around. Perhaps if she married him, our troubles would be over.

Spain was my ancestral home. For as long as 1 could remember, I'd been told about the purity of my Spanish blood. 1 wasn't Cuban, but rather a victim of my birthplace. Why not return home at last, even if 1 didn't know where any of my relatives lived, or who they were? Clearly, moving to

Spain could be the start of a whole new life. Why fret over it? If I didn't like it there, I'd use it as a steppingstone to the States.

America—that was the real prize. The land where everyone was blond, blue-eyed, and rich. Yes, America was the place with streets paved in gold, where everyone had jobs and lived in great big houses protected by quaint white picket fences and manicured green lawns. I wanted to be rich and live in one of those houses. I wanted to be famous and for all my friends to be beautiful blonds because I secretly had always wanted to be blond.

Still, Mother had been wrong to inform me of her decision without even asking me first. I had a mind, a voice, and things I needed to say. Things I was entitled to say.

She had injured me, and I was too prideful to apologize for blowing up at her because I knew she'd never apologize to me. Yet, I saw that she was right, and that life could be better in Spain. Secure in my decision, I returned home but didn't share my decision with her until the end of the day. The relief on her face was obvious, and I was glad that I'd worried her. God knows she deserved a bit of her own medicine.

TRUCE

Our common cause and mutual drive forced Mother and me to work together. There was no sense in wasting time arguing over details when there was so much that needed to be arranged.

There were birth certificates to gather and passports to apply for. There were letters to cousins, relatives, and friends, begging or shaming them into wiring us the more than $300 in passage money that we each needed to present our claim. There were visas at the Spanish embassy to obtain. And there was the day when the authorities came to conduct a full inventory of everything we owned because becoming a *gusano*—a worm who abandons the cause—meant that every glass, plate, knife, and fork belonged thereafter to the people and the revolution, and not to us anymore.

Overnight, everyone knew. The world turned into competing camps between those who were staying behind and sympathized but kept away in fear, and those who hated our cause and belittled us at every turn.

Then the block's revolutionary committee began its patrols, where one individual or another walked by the house at all hours of the day and night, asking for the name of any visitor whose face they didn't recognize. And there was the talk in the principal's office at school, where I was told that I was being watched so that everything I did and said could be reported to those who kept the records of our case.

Long months of waiting were to follow without ever hearing a word. Panic-filled months of knowing that they could stop us from leaving over something as trivial as me thinking the wrong thought. Endless months of knowing that even something as simple as a missing dish could bring the dream to its end on the day the departure orders arrived, and the final inventory was conducted again.

Underneath the calm façade I presented to the world, I was panicking. What if the orders didn't arrive before I turned fifteen? Then I'd have to wait a decade before asking again for permission to leave. How does anyone survive in a world where they are neither wanted nor free?

ANGELS

Mother's turn came long before mine. Her turn came in the early spring of 1968, and there was nothing she could have done or said to save herself from the humiliation and pain. Her only choice was to get up in the middle of the night, get ready, and walk the blocks to the corner where all the worms—forced to work in the fields rather than vegetate or *take*, as the government repeatedly said—gathered in a huddle until the army truck came. Then they stood face-to-face, back-to-back, a mass of anxious flesh on the back of the open truck. Once they reached their destination, they labored until dusk.

Some days, the work was light labor such as picking tomatoes from under the vines that stretched from ridge to ridge, their ripening fruit hanging low in the furrow's cool breast. Then there were the days when they faced endless sugar cane fields where men and women alike were expected to cut and clean the stalks with the machetes they gripped in their hands.

The food was rationed, and its availability uncertain, for no one ever knew, from one day to the next, when it would arrive or what it would be. And even when it did appear, most often it was but a limited supply of boiled sweet potatoes (*boniatos*) served without bread, knives, or forks. The water was rationed as well, carried to the fields in buckets by the peasant men who supervised. And of course, bathroom breaks took place in full display of everyone. Through it all, government officials happily vegetated from their shelter in the shade. All this was as it had been intended to be: to humiliate, destroy, and deny. Just as before the revolution, the peasants worked and the oppressed starved while those with power or connection exploited them. Batista may have no longer been in power, but nothing had changed.

Nonetheless, the saying goes that God offers us what we need rather than what we may want. This was the case when a new worker named Anita recognized Mother. *"Pero, Margarita, ¿No te acuerdas de mí? ¿No te recuerdas que nos conocimos en el cabaré?"* Don't you remember me from the cabaret? But Mother didn't remember until Anita told her that she was the makeup artist and hairdresser at the nightclub where Valentín most often performed. Mother's memory jogged, she did remember her, and from that moment on, the two women looked out for one another at every turn. Anita lived eight blocks from us, but they had never met except for those nights at the club.

Discovering their proximity to one another, they spent their free Sundays together, relaxing, and sympathizing with one another's plight in life. They became good friends, and I was introduced to Anita and her cousin Mariana, who lived with her. It didn't take me long to figure out what was going on behind closed doors. As with Nenico and Antonio, their stolen glances, and all-knowing smiles were a dead giveaway as to their sexual orientation.

Welcoming me into their lives, they made it clear that they were understanding friends I could trust. Both had applied in the hopes of leaving together for Spain, but Mariana had evaded working at the labor camps because she'd been able to convince the authorities that she was an unstable diabetic who could faint or die from strenuous labor. Helped by every family member and friend, even the block's revolutionary committee was fooled. Quietly, and with every eye on the lookout, she ran a hair and nail salon from their house.

Had Mother known their secret? She never spoke about it. Had this been the reason she so violently insisted that I never again visit Nenico and Antonio? Was she afraid that I was like them? Was she wise to me? It would have been just like Sebastián's aunt to blame me for his actions. Was I to blame for her pushing Miguel out of the house? It would make sense because he walked away, and I never saw him again.

But I hadn't the time to wallow in guilt with so many pressing matters to deal with in my quest to get to Spain. That had to be my focus, and nothing else, if we were going to succeed. Instead of beating myself up over the past, which I had no control over, I rejoiced at discovering two incredible women who enjoyed my company, my wit, and charm. Two women in the same boat as me. Two women who would encourage and guide me at every turn. In the hands of Anita and Mariana, I refined my talents for charming with subtle smiles and glances. With their support, my confidence grew. I convinced myself that I could jump and outmaneuver any obstacle tossed in my path. I'd survived bullies on the playground, condescending teachers and wicked priests, judgmental neighbors, abusive men I thought loved me, an absentee father, a monster mother, and being mocked for what I was. By comparison, escaping to Spain seemed a manageable quest.

RECKONING

My turn at laboring came in the early summer of 1968. At the end of the school year, the boys and the girls in my secondary school were separated, loaded onto buses, and driven out of the city to work in the fields. For hours, our bus drove west into the Pinar del Río province, which I had visited once with Tía Cecilia during a class trip when I was four. But we were not going to visit Viñales. Our destination was a grouping of hastily built barracks surrounded by miles of sugar cane fields.

I may have dreamed about an ideal life at the farm, but I'd never worked in a field in my life.

Looking out the window of the bus, I escaped into the beauty of a countryside that was quite different from my own province's landscape. In the distance, majestic mountains rested atop rolling valleys of red earth. Tobacco groves rose tall to meet a periwinkle blue sky adorned with simple cotton balls. The green vegetation glistened in the morning light as if had been dusted with gold.

Secondary school had been both joyous and terrifying. I'd learned to curb my enthusiastic behavior by then. By not showing off and not plowing over others to be the first with the correct answer, I acquiesced to others, and fortunately, no longer angered my teachers and classmates. I shielded my vulnerability with wit. Self-deprecating humor and quick retorts baffled the bullies and spared me altercations. Nonetheless, fear was a constant companion for me.

Advantageously, starting in fourth grade, 1 was afforded a reprise from the bullies, who'd set their cap on easier prey than me, all because an effeminate boy we all called Pipo followed me from one class to the next. Whenever the boys gathered to tease him or beat up on him, 1 quietly slipped away, just in case 1, too, would fall victim to them. Like the girls who ran to his rescue, 1 should've defended him, but 1 was terrified of the bullies who battered him. Although I'd avoided the bruises, kicks, and cuts he suffered, 1 felt their impact because 1 saw myself in him.

Seeing Pipo's bloody body lying still on the ground, 1 realized that a single misstep on my part, and I'd end up stretched out beside him. So when it came time to go to Pinar del Río province, 1 feared spending weeks together with my schoolmates and having no place to hide. To silence the trembling of my terrified mind, I'd convinced myself that Pipo would continue to be the recipient of all the boys' punishment.

Blinded by fear, 1 hadn't noticed that the episodes of harassment had diminished by the time we'd transferred to our secondary school. Little did 1 know that Pipo had willingly been satisfying their demands. How could 1 have known; I'd never seen him beyond the schoolyard. 1 didn't see any of this until the day 1 walked into the building lined up with latrines, and saw the long line of boys waiting for a turn with him.

In the flash of a moment, my confidence and resolve withered away. 1 worried that my desires and aggressive nature might drive me to compete with Pipo. Part of me longed to take my place next to him—all my careful planning and my well-rehearsed games abandoning me right there and then.

But why not join in, I asked myself? Why not simply join in? After all, these boys were not there to inflict insults or the bodily harm that I had dreaded night and day. These boys were as if insects trapped in a spider's web, and they no longer seemed strong, but weak to me. Besides, I had handled weak men many times before. How difficult could it be for me to handle these boys?

Somehow, I restrained my wild imagination. Instead, I watched from the shadows and took copious mental notes of Pipo's every move and his prowess at pleasing each boy in line. Without doubt, he was much more experienced than me, and I was eager to learn.

I must have stared at the proceedings for too long because three boys caught on and forced me to my knees before I had a chance to think or beg.

I wanted to join in. I wanted nothing more than to join in. But I froze in fear and refused to play, even when they shoved my face into their crotch.

Suddenly, a feeding frenzy ensued when the three boys invited other boys to the party. The bodily harm that for so many years I had worked hard to evade, now engulfed me in abuse.

Through foggy eyes, I looked up at my school principal kneeling over me as he directed the officials to gently lift and carry me to the nurse's hut. As they did, my entire body shattered into a thousand miniscule pieces of splintered bones and ripped flesh.

Despite the pain pulsing through every fraction of me, they assured me that no bones had been broken. And to my disbelief, I thanked the God I believed had abandoned me, for keeping me safe. My swollen lips and tongue made it impossible to eat or drink. For many days, I stayed there at the nurse's hut, nurturing my wounds and my pride.

In my welcomed repose, I gazed out the window and marveled at the rich red earth and golden growth sprouting from deep in its soul. My face against the window, the warm sunlight nourished me.

As the weekend neared, I was told that Mother would arrive to take me home. This news embraced me with relief. I looked forward to the anticipated safety.

The dorm where all the teachers, officials, and boys lived and slept stood atop a gentle hill. At its front, a dirt clearing allowed the buses filled with visiting relatives to park. At its back, the ground sloped away to the nurse's hut before continuing to the showers, latrines, and eventually the great mess hall where the cooks were busy preparing a special meal to impress those visiting that day. Two racks stood in the sun, and a roasting pig was laid on top of each one.

Sitting at the door of the nurse's hut, I could smell the citrus and spices carried on the lazy breeze, and I closed my eyes to dream of *la finca* and its sweet-scented black earth, of Mamá's smiling zinnias farm, of the day Father and I shared the roasted ear of corn—back to the world when I was only six. I kept my eyes closed until I sensed the cool shadow of someone blocking the sun. When I opened them, Mother was towering over me. Cupping my hands into a visor, I stared at her, expecting to see a glimmer of concern, a kind smile, or a pensive expression. The mother standing before me, her arms crossed over her chest, was stiff-lipped and angry, reproach written on her face. The woman standing there was the same creature who had been clutching the kitchen table when I was three. Suddenly I was three again, and all at once, the strength I had gained through rest and sunlight abandoned me.

Then I was no longer sitting on the chair bathed in sunlight, but atop our kitchen table, next to a shimmering knife. I lowered my eyes and looked away. I refused to let her zap what little strength I had, because she was a parasite consumed by shame. There was ever only room in her heart, sympathy in her soul, for one person—herself.

On the bus ride home, I sat with my loaded homemade backpack on my lap across the aisle from Mother. In the taxi on our way home, I kept the backpack between us.

The house, locked up and empty, seemed abandoned when we arrived. Los tíos, wishing to stay as far away from Mother's rage as they could, ran away to stay with Papá and Mamá. It was only the two of us inside the house.

"*Espera hasta que se lo diga a tu padre.*" Wait until I tell your father, she said, knowing that was the one tool at her disposal that could hurt me the most.

"*¡Escúchame, Margarita!*" Listen to me! I said, and she lowered her eyes. She grimaced when I called her by her name. It was a deliberate act of defiance, a signal that she had crossed the line, and a sign of my diminishing love for her. Her eyes glazed over. She seemed desolate and lost, but I refused to give in. I wasn't about to lower my guard. I was focused on the task ahead. To give in would've weakened my position, and position was one of the few tools left in my arsenal.

"*¿Quieres pelear? ¿Está segura? ¡Entonces peleamos! ¿Qué quieres? ¿Que salga corriendo a la calle y decirles a todos que mala madre tu fuistes? ¿Debo decirles a todos que duermes en la misma cama con Valentín?*" You want to fight? Are you sure? Then we fight! What do you want? Do you want me to run out into the street and tell everyone what a bad mother you were? Should I tell everyone that you sleep in the same bed with Valentín?

I was ready to wage war on her if fighting for that ounce of respect Father had for me would keep him from knowing the truth.

I'd shocked her. Thinking me vulnerable, she wasn't prepared for my fighting back nor speaking the truth.

I could not endure the thought of Father walking out of my life once again. I could not bear the thought of never being able to hold Tomás in my arms again.

In a moment when I needed her compassion, she drenched me with cruelty.

That night, we retreated to our rooms to avoid the minefield between us. One false move and one of us would end up in a heap upon the floor.

Mother pulled out her old bag of tricks the next morning and pretended our rift had never happened. She treated me as if I were a small child, showering me with hugs and kisses, sweeping her bad behavior under the rug. Onto her game, I coldly ignored her attempt at affection. She didn't fool me.

Unable to apologize, she nonetheless, silently laid the gauntlet at me feet. Victory, even if momentary, was mine. Now empowered, I reaped the benefit of standing up for myself, and realized that it could be a winning strategy for me. However, my fear persisted, and since Father thought I was away, I didn't visit him for several weeks. I felt safe in the knowledge that Mother was too fearful to tell.

Departures

Valentín's orders came on a hot August day, and we celebrated the news on a Sunday, in solemn silence from behind the closed door of our house. The facts were simple: Mother wouldn't be able to be at the airport with him because she worked all week in the fields, and I wouldn't be allowed to travel to the airport by myself. The exposure was too dangerous.

It must have been difficult for him to be all alone at the airport without any relatives by his side. Claiming to be a native of the eastern most province of Oriente, easily nearly twenty hours away by bus, we had never met anyone from his family, and only knew the few details he'd been willing to share with us. He spoke of an aunt in Queens, New York, who could not wait to see him again, but not much else. Still, he'd been good to us and had introduced us to a new world and a new life, and we loved him for all he'd done. Mother and I had been eager to believe, and hungry to trust someone.

Besides, thanks to him, we'd met Anita and Mariana, who made everything bearable. With them, I was happy with my life. Hanging around their beauty shop was a joy, and I'd learned to care less about Mother's feeling or her opinions. Her moods ran hot and cold and were unpredictable, at best. She'd flip from one act to another when the present didn't yield the desired results. Mother was nothing more than a Chameleon changing its colors as she jumped from branch to branch. And like Tía Cecilia, I didn't care to see the subtle changes that swept across her face from one moment to the next.

We all chose to ignore the sad, quiet days she moped about the house, feeling sorry for herself. So I left her alone when she took to speaking to no one. Actually, it was relief not having to deal with her anxiously pacing the floors or watching her fly into a rage at the drop of a hat.

Anita's and Mariana's orders came on a wet October day, and we gathered at their house to say our goodbyes. My days at the hair salon ended with their departure, and I anxiously waited for our orders to come. On sunny days, I was certain they'd soon arrive. And when the clouds rolled in, doubt and fear would grip me. I resorted to prayer, papering over my sorrow and loss with hope. Fear is overwhelming, and I was easily overwhelmed by it. What if our orders never came? What if I never again got to visit with the girls or see Valentín?

Our orders did come. They arrived on a chilly December day, and we rushed to the Iberia Airlines office to buy the one-way ticket for our flight without delay. That was the big price—being able to leave the county not on a Cuban propeller flight where we would still be under the authorities' control until landing in Spain. All that people wished for was to get a ticket on either KLM—the Dutch airline—or Iberia— the Spanish airline. Their jet planes represented freedom and a symbol of capitalism's endless might. It all felt empowering somehow, knowing that we had secured such a treat.

From that moment until our departure, Mother's mood turned into an overflowing river of aspiration as she rushed to get ready and pack the things that she had been able to get or make, all to ensure that we would arrive in Madrid not looking like the poor refugees we were, but rather travelers who could demand respect from strangers in Spain. As a happy surprise, the officials never returned to inventory the contents of the house after so much worrying and pain.

Valentín had been a diligent writer, and we knew that there was an apartment waiting for us, just like we knew that both Anita and Mariana had been occupying the same apartment since arriving in Madrid. They were waiting for us! What else could we want?

Mother quickly wrote to all the cousins and friends in the States to share the news and our new address, hoping that their many checks and dollars would be there waiting for us.

I wasn't sad during that last Sunday spent with Father, Zoraida, and baby Tomás. How could I be? They, too, had moved ahead with their plans and were anxiously waiting for their orders to leave, not through Spain, but through Mexico, which guaranteed a much faster passage to the States. I felt confident that we would be together again soon, not understanding the great distances between Miami, where they planned to live, and Queens, where Valentín planned to be.

In the morning, Father, Zoraida, baby Tomás, and I went to the zoo, which had always been a place I loved, even if I seldom took the time to go. Then it was back to their working-class Cerro neighborhood apartment for a late lunch and a nap. I remember Tomás sleeping on his stomach with his right leg crossed over his left, and Father pointing out that both he and I also crossed our legs when we slept. I remember looking at Father with the same eyes I had used to look at him during our magic *guaguita* ride when I was six. I remember feeling that my life was complete.

Our departure was scheduled only days before my fifteenth birthday, which would mark the day when I'd no longer be permitted to leave. I lived with the fear that something could go wrong, and our flight would be postponed.

On that day, the house was brimming with everyone who came to say goodbye: Papá, Mamá, the uncles and aunts, even Cousin Nicolás. Just as they had done almost four years earlier on the day of the big *la finca* move, they clustered in small groups, displaying little warmth, as if their physical presence were somehow enough. Unlike that day, I now understood their coldness because I, too, behaved as they behaved. Indifference was the only tool at our disposal as we struggled to cope with the inevitable pain and loss.

It had been a frightening start, arriving at the airport for our early evening flight, only to be separated by sex before being asked to strip naked for a physical search where each orifice was methodically probed to make sure we were not concealing any contraband. After that, we sat in unspoken panic, waiting for the plane to arrive.

We all walked single file toward the sleek DC-8. The air was crisp, and the late-afternoon cloudless sky was bright. There was no breeze. Overhead, a speaker played a Russian communist march.

Anticipated freedom encouraged every step we took. No one looked back, in fear of disobeying the orders and being detained.

I took a step and then another step, until reaching the top of the staircase, where I stood on its narrow platform for an unnoticeable second to defiantly look back before crossing the metal threshold.

Then the moment came when the airplane's door closed, and I knew that such a thud was the physical confirmation of no return.

I avoided the pain by simply choosing not to mourn what I had left. Instead, I fabricated my own private dreams out of spun sugar and meringue—which are fragile, at best—but felt safe because I had carefully wrapped them in hope. Hope bound by ribbons of imagined good fortunes and miracles still to come.

LIBERATION

I woke up to an unfamiliar Castilian lisp, and when I opened my eyes, the slim stewardess placed a steaming washcloth in my hand. She was dressed in the reds, oranges, and golds of the Spanish flag as if to complement the colors inside the airplane. It was then that the captain bid us all good morning and announced that we would soon be approaching land and flying over Portugal. In anticipation, I reached for the little window at my left, lifted up the shade, and welcomed the piercing sunlight.

It had been such a magical flight, and the meal the previous evening had amazed everyone. Eight-inch shrimp atop chipped ice and served with spicy red sauce, round pork medallions, roasted potatoes, and a salad to the one side, steaming bread to soak up the rich gravy, cake and custard for dessert, as much water, soda, coffee, tea, and juice as we liked—all this and more, followed by a restful night's sleep while wrapped in freedom's perfect arms.

Still, the mood inside the DC-8 had remained strangely subdued. I had expected for a plane filled with always-vocal Cuban people to break out into song and chant the minute we had taken off. Instead, people seemed rather numb, almost as if the contraband probes had injected us with too much trauma to celebrate, or left us unable to let go. Perhaps each passenger was quietly fabricating their own merengue dreams, as I had done.

Regardless of the cause, I, too, found myself unable to understand, or even express, how I felt. Sitting next to me,

Mother's face displayed no sadness or regret. Rather, her eyes smiled like a child's eyes smile when sitting down to devour a great big dessert.

The sun pierced through the cold, and I was happy for the warmth of its kiss as I walked down the ramp and into the back of the little shuttle bus. Once inside the airport, our papers and luggage were reviewed and checked with a friendly politeness that made me feel safe. Surely this kindness was but an example of what lay ahead for us in Spain. Walking away from everything had been the right thing.

Inside Barajas Airport, wide, shiny halls traveled in all directions while metal waves flowed high above. There, a well-fed Cuban lady joined our group and boarded the bus to instruct us on the events that came next. She was dressed in an orange and black plaid suit, and her blouse hid her short neck behind a huge lemon cake bow.

Once on the multi-lane highway, I could see silver hills sparkling in the morning sun, fading away as we got close to the city, and gray clouds rolled in to obscure the bright light.

From my window, I saw one broad avenue after the next, each lined with tall and intricately chiseled façades reminiscent of Havana's Teatro Gallego, where I had been so happy with Mother and Valentín.

Little black cars came and went, and I wondered how it was possible for anyone to fit inside of them. These were not the great tail-finned cars that I loved so much; these were not much bigger than a young child's pedal car.

It was early morning, and people hurried in all directions, but were clearly sure of their final goal. Packs of students strolled their way to school, dressed in pleated skirts and tan pants while wearing navy blazers or coats, and all I wanted to do was wrap myself in one of their long woolen striped scarves covering their faces and throats. All at once, snowflakes floated through the air, only to melt as soon as they landed on the student's dark clothes. I hadn't expected them to do that. I didn't know how fragile they were.

The bus came to a stop in front of a gray stone building that our guide addressed as an American Protestant church. There, we marched to its basement and entered a large open hall. Its plaster walls were an indescribable shade of pale green because the harsh fluorescent light had washed away their color. At the far end, a group of even more dignified Cuban ladies sat behind long tables piled with papers and forms.

One by one, we stood in line once again to have our documents examined, and to receive further instructions on what needed to be done. No one in the arriving crowd seemed too interested in any of this because we were all too busy looking around and then looking for the friends and relatives waiting for us. No reunion was to take place until we had all been taken to a smaller room with racks and tables of donated clothes, and we were instructed to take just one of each.

Mother, broadcasting that her wool pant suit was enough, refused to even look or take anything because she didn't want to wear other people's used things. As for me, I eagerly searched and searched until finding a long camel-colored coat with a wide collar and lapels, which I knew was the right thing. I was surprised by how heavy it was.

Not until then were we allowed to walk into the next room to be welcomed by the crowd's cheers and applause. Only then did I find myself able to feel anything, as if the presence of those we knew and loved had acted as an antidote to the numbness that we had all been poisoned with at Havana's airport.

My heart jumped into many somersaults the moment I saw Anita and Valentín waiting there for us! I felt such relief knowing that I was at last free.

Every nerve in my body seemed to fire at once, and I could feel the emotions in the room. I could smell each cologne and perfume floating in the air. I could hear every breath and heartbeat. Never had I felt or seen so much love in one space. I stood there soaking it all in, feeling alive and recharged.

For me, arriving in Spain meant so much more than freedom from the oppression and the laboring camp. This new autonomy meant that I was free to be anything and become anyone. I no longer needed to worry about the bullying or the punishment. I no longer needed to be bound by my years of sitting on unshaven men's laps. I no longer needed to care about the judging church ladies rolling their eyes while working their fans. I was free to put away my feelings for Miguel and my regrets towards Sebastián. Free to forget about Padre Felipe and his deceit.

All that had come before was finally in the past. I was like a young bird jumping out of its nest to enjoy the pleasure of its virgin flight.

GLUTTONY

Anita and I eagerly watched as Mother and Valentín pulled away in a taxi for a brief holiday. I was relieved not having to worry about her. I wanted to think about me. I was ecstatic because Anita and I were together again. I could not wait to be by Mariana's side. I could not wait to get home and start my new life.

Together, we made an interesting band. We were like a three-legged stool which has surprising sturdiness despite its unconventional construction. I suppose that Mother could have been considered the fourth leg, but we never really needed her support.

Anita resembled her father, a short, round *gallego*, but with a square rather than round face. Marianna's frame, in turn, was much more like the typical Cuban woman's frame, with abundant breasts, a small waste, ample hips and thighs. Unlike Anita, whose paleness had returned after no longer working in the fields, Marianna's skin was a deep color perhaps best described as *dulce de leche* because it was much lighter than cinnamon and had the creamy richness of caramel. Both being working-class *habaneras*, they spoke with the traditional tones, which were always more clipped than Mother's guajira sing-song. Their accent was comforting in its directness and strength. Anita was thirty-eight and Mariana forty-one.

❧

Calle del Mesón de Paredes in the neighborhood of Lavapiés was no more than a noisy, narrow stone lane with even narrower sidewalks. As such, the taxi driver could only push forward at a crawl while constantly tooting his horn. Only this insistent sound and proximity to our car could reluctantly urge the people to squeeze back onto the sidewalks. As soon as we passed, the crowd rushed back out onto the street.

On either side, grocery stores, a pharmacy, a general store, and many other stores enticed the people to step in to browse and to shop. However, by the large number of bars and people in them, even at midday, it was easy to assume that many went to this part of town to party and drink. As we passed each bar, thunderous waves of voices and rolling laughter spilled onto the street to engulf our car in their contagious tumult.

At one bar, three prostitutes gathered as if they owned the road and the sidewalk. I knew about prostitutes from the times I visited Father near Calle Ánimas, because this was the location of the *pollería* where he worked. Mother always demanded that I not visit him there because of such element, but I had become too independent to listen to her. Besides, the ladies I met around his store were all gifted with a snappy sense of humor I certainly enjoyed, even if their jokes were very often delivered with a *chusma* undertone. My ego certainly enjoyed them praising my beauty when they held my face in their hands, as if I were a deity to be kissed and adored. "*Ay, mira, que guapo,*" they used to say. Still, the thought of these new *madrileñas* not seeing my sexual indifference toward them was frightening for me. Receiving pleasant praises back in Cuba from the other ladies was one thing, but being seen as prey now was a truly disgusting thing. Fearful of such moments, I decided never to acknowledge them whenever I passed one on the street.

Our apartment building presented a handsome face not unlike that of the many buildings around Calle Ánimas, or even the buildings at the wide plaza surrounding the old Havana cathedral, which was hundreds of years old. And like almost every other building on Mesón de Paredes, the rows of iron balconies on each of our building's three floors had been adorned with a multitude of empty terracotta pots and laundry hung to dry. All of this felt more familiar that strange. I felt a happy thrill knowing that this collection of balconied buildings, stores, bars, and even prostitutes, all competing for attention within the confines of such a narrow street, was going to be my new home.

An oversized honey-colored carved door squeaked and slowly creaked aside to show a short landing big enough to hold my suitcase, Anita, and me. In front of us, a staircase with warped and worn steps guided us to the floors above.

The short vestibule, with its cloudy mirror and an old telephone hanging on the wall, smelled musty and dank. However, there was no time to think about the smell or the décor, because the second we opened the door, Mariana rushed up to meet us, and then the three of us stood there locked in a long embrace.

In time, Anita pointed out the delicately frosted glass doors leading to two bedrooms facing the streets, but I didn't go in to look at my room. Instead, I followed them down a narrow dark hall, enticed by the bright rays of light streaming into the next room. I stopped suddenly at the dining room's threshold because I felt as if I had been there before.

A table twin to the one in my childhood's magical kitchen kingdom stood in the middle of the room. Even the upright black leather chairs were the same. And the small white refrigerator and yellow walls seemed the same.

All this familiarity made me wonder what kind of bowl this new home would be. Perhaps a simple bowl serving a rich stew, as when I was three. Maybe a shiny metal bowl filled with juicy red grapes to be pealed and eaten one at a time. It certainly would never be like Mother's *pollería* where everything existed to ferment and rot.

The noise from the street below welcomed me the moment I entered my bedroom at the front of the house. An old oak armchair stood in front of a window, and I placed my suitcase by its side. A solitary bed stood in the middle of the room. This, along with a nightstand and lamp, worked hard to fill the room's great size.

I wasn't tired, but tried to lay down and rest while the 200 *pesetas* (about $3.00) that Valentín had given me begged to be spent. I could not rest; there was too much I wanted to see and feel. I just wanted to run out into the street. So I asked Anita for my keys and flew out into the street.

I stood in front of the grocery store's windows, completely overtaken by the heaping displays of hams, sausages, cheeses, fruits, and breads. I stood there examining everything until I knew exactly what I wanted to get.

I was amazed by how much my money had been able to buy. Boundless satisfaction escorted me as I rushed back home, and I didn't stop until landing on the bed with my legs crossed.

Enthusiastically, I opened the brown paper package to examine my treats before swiftly devouring the shiny red apple and the great chunk of yellow cheese without stopping to take a single breath. Only then, while feeling so alive, did I allow sleep to enter the room and hold my hand, just as the smiling naked boy had once done in *los abuelito's* living room.

I wasted no time the next morning and dashed out of the house, ready to investigate. I wanted to smell every smell. I wanted to look at and touch everything. I wanted to listen to every word that people spoke. I wanted to see how they dressed, moved, and walked.

The prior day's clouds and snow were gone, and the sun shined brightly as I walked the six blocks along Mesón de Paredes, until it opened into a triangular-shaped plaza named Tirso de Molina, where I saw a metro station entrance for the very first time.

Such a magnificent thing, a set of steep stairs going down deep into the ground, leading to trains which could take me anywhere I wanted to go.

ABANDONMENT

Mother and Valentín both seemed unusually quiet when they walked into the dining room three days after our arrival, and we were sure that they hadn't wed. She'd bragged about this taking place the moment of our arrival in Spain. Did he tell her that he was leaving for the States in less than a week? I hadn't known about this until that morning, when Anita and Mariana told me. We were all terrified because we knew that Mother would not have reacted well to such news. So before Mother could say anything, Mariana handed her a pack of letters and her face lit up because every person she'd written to had sent her either money or a check.

The rest of the week passed in silence as we all continued to play the game. Mother and Valentín explained nothing, and we never inquired about their plans because we didn't know how to ask the question in a manner that wouldn't have Mother explode. So we said nothing. Even on our way back from the airport, after saying goodbye to Valentín, Mother never explained, and we three wondered what her silence meant.

Days turned into weeks of suspended stalemate. Mother wrote daily to Valentín and waited for his letters, as well as those from relatives she was convinced would continue sending money to us.

I wasn't there when the letter arrived, and didn't hear anything until I opened the door and walked down the hall.

In the dining room sat women in rollers, and others with their hair teased high. One woman was letting the brightest shade of red dye set in. But the screams! The awful noise of Mother screaming coming from the bathroom.

I walked in measured steps through the open-shelved kitchen, to the bathroom, and peeked in. Inside, Anita was holding Mother under the rushing water. Flailing about, Mother stood, fully clothed, waling, bawling, and complaining that the shower water was ice cold. "*¿Para qué? ¿Para que yo me fui? ¡Y que pasara ahora que yo no voy a estar allá para cerrar los ojos de mi madre!*" For what? Why did I leave? And what is to happen now that I'll not be there to close my mother's eyes!

Again, and again, Mother kept screaming the same thing. When Anita noticed me frozen in the threshold, she insisted that I get out and send Mariana in.

As we passed in the kitchen, Mariana handed me a crumpled letter and a check, but my hands were shaking so badly, I couldn't read it. So one of the women kindly took it from me and guided me to a chair. One by one, she read each word as if it had been the paced drum beat at a funeral march:

Margarita

No me escribas más por favor. Tú me pediste asistencia para sacar tu hijo de Cuba y yo te lo di. Pero yo quiero tener mis hijos también y eso no es posible contigo. Aquí te mando un cheque por $300 dólares pero es lo último que te puedo mandar.

—Valentín

Margarita

Please do not write to me anymore. You asked
me for assistance to get your son out of Cuba,
and I gave it to you. But I also want to have
my own children, and this is not possible with
you. I have included a check for $300 dollars,
but this is the last money I can send.

—Valentín

I sat there unable to move, and fixed my gaze on the
old credenza on the back wall, where half-empty bottles of
sherry and rum competed for a place with the hairbrushes,
combs, rollers, and pins. I dropped my head in my hands
and stared at the floor before lifting it, and in slow motion,
looked at every woman across the room. They were all silent.
The sheer curtain before the window hung from a sagging
brass rod, moved up and down like a shriveling shroud, rising
and falling, its hem puffed up like a wide-mouth frog. The
sun had surrendered to the gray clouds.

In a crushing silence, the ladies and I watched Anita
and Mariana walk Mother down the hall to her room, and
in unison, breathed in the profound sadness the cloudy
shadows had carried in. The familiar sense of loss I foolishly
thought had disappeared from my life weighed as heavy on
my heart as on the day I watched Papá drive away from the
empty house in August of 1965. Nothing had changed.

That evening, as Mother hid in her room, medicated
from the round, magical yellow pills one of the women had
left behind, Anita, Mariana, and I huddled around the dining
table, holding hands and racking our brains to come up with
some sort of plan—an urgent plan, since all four of us had
depended on Valentín's money to survive. I volunteered to
move into the small windowless pantry that opened into the
dining room. This meant we could rent my room. Still, this
would not bring enough money to cover all the bills.

And what about food? What would we do about food? Mother had made it clear that she was never going to leave her room again, and we three agreed to humor her until she recovered from the shock.

Two of us could walk to the soup kitchen for our one meal of the day, while the third one kept an eye on Mother. However, she needed to eat, and Mariana's diabetes required her to eat more than one meal a day. Somehow, we needed to find a way to keep food in the house.

Without any preparation or warning, I had become the man of the house, and I took on the duty of keeping everyone safe.

AN EMPTY BOWL

Doña Catalina wasn't quite through the door before introducing herself as *una dama muy digna*, meaning a lady of great dignity. She then went on to make sure we knew about her aristocratic pedigree, and that she was waiting to unite with her husband and children in the States. We rented her my room the moment she flashed cash because she didn't question the high price.

I'd told myself that moving into the narrow, windowless pantry room didn't worry me at all. That I did what needed to be done. That it didn't matter because I'd be too busy exploring my new world. That I'd be gone for hours at my fabulous first job. That giving up my bright room would not be such an awful sacrifice because the sun broke through the dining room's window only steps away.

A series of built-in shelves ran up one wall, and a folded cot had been shoved against the other wall. Except for an old wooden crate stuffed with a pillow, sheets, and blankets inside, there was only a small lamp that stood on the floor next it. A solitary light bulb hung from the middle of the ceiling high above, but its light was too dim to let the shadows free themselves from the walls.

I sat there on the open cot, staring at the lamp. I sat there not blinking, but just staring at the crack across its plastic shade. I sat there recalling the path that had brought me to that moment and place. I sat there recalling my happy days in my yellow kitchen kingdom and my big boy room with my own perfect headboard. I sat there trying to forget my *pollería* vestibule room with its own lamp on the floor, and all the smells and the chickens fighting day and night. I sat there hating what my life had become. I sat there not willing to accept that this pantry would be my home for as long as I lived in Spain. I sat there until Mariana walked into the room, sat next to me, and held me close. I sat with my head on her heart until I found the strength to get up and walk.

Breakdown

By early April, the weary Madrid winter of 1969 had surrendered to spring. Like everyone else, I was happy that the morning arrived earlier every day. The prostitutes next door were wearing their flame-red or platinum-teased mops, and as a salute to spring, painted their lips bright coral and their eyelids a brilliant robin-egg blue. Without their coats, they all seemed slimmer in the shortest skits I'd ever seen.

Next to Doña Catalina's room, Mother stayed behind her locked bedroom door, refusing to come out. When she was certain that no one was awake, she'd leave long frantic letters, her handwriting becoming less legible by the day, on the hall table for me to mail the next morning. Thinking she was fooling us, she'd scurry to the bathroom to empty her chamber pot and raid the refrigerator and kitchen for something to eat. Little did she know that we were on to her. This routine became a nightly ritual.

From behind our closed doors, which opened to the dining room, we heard her talking to Valentín as if he were there. On and on she'd go, fighting and pleading with a man thousands of miles away. Then, as fast as it began, it was over and she'd tiptoe back to her room and lock herself in. The situation was getting worse, and we were at a loss as to what we could or should do with her.

One night, Anita surprised her, cornering her in the kitchen, attempting to convince her to face facts and get on with her life: "*Mira para eso. ¿Oye, no te das cuentas que tienes un niño? ¿Como es eso posible? Vamos, entra al baño ahora mismo para que entonces mañana empieces a buscar algún trabajo."* Reminding her she was a parent with a child to support, Anita implored her to clean herself up and go out to look for a job the next day.

But Mother said, *"Ay no, no puedo. ¡Déjame! ¡Déjame!"* She screamed that she could not, and begged to be left alone. Dropping to the floor, she crawled like a baby back to her room and slammed the door so hard that the picture hanging on the foyer wall went cockeyed. Standing on the other side, we watched her shadow against the frosted glass door sitting on the floor. Her arms wrapped around herself, she rocked back and forth.

For the remainder of the night, Mother sobbed, cursed, and complained about her life: Father's adultery, his accusations about my conception, never having a doll of her own, being sent away at fourteen years old, her mother never being affectionate with her. The more she bellowed and bawled, the less sympathy I felt. The more she babbled, the more disgusted I became. I detested her selfish rants and her unapologetic lack of concern for me.

I hated everything about her. She was unable or unwilling to cope. She sang the same tired songs I'd heard since I was born, and I was exhausted by the burdens she handed to me like a pair of worn-out shoes.

I hated her controlling my life from the other side of a locked door. I hated her for subjecting me to senseless cruelty. She wasn't one to suffer silently on her own. If she were hurting, then so would those around her. Especially me.

REGRETS

Anita and I met a small group of Cubans at Tirso de Molina plaza only six blocks from the house. From there, we all zig-zagged through the little streets until reaching Plaza de las Cortes, where the big group waited for us. Then we walked the few blocks to the soup kitchen in the middle of a narrow side street. It was just past ten in the morning, but a long line was already waiting for us.

From across the street, a pack of men walked back and forth while hurtling insults at us. I didn't understand why they kept crying about Cubans being fed while they and their families had nothing to eat. Our crowd simply dismissed their laments, and worried about not fitting in, I was hesitant to ask anyone why.

Inside, a narrow room had been taken over by long wooden tables already set up with simple white soup plates, utensils, glasses, and large water glasses. At the far end, the smell from the kitchen enticed everyone to quickly sit in order for the feast to begin.

Eagerly, we waited for the stout peasant women to place their large steaming pots of *caldo gallego*—a hearty white bean soup seasoned with onion and garlic and loaded with potatoes, turnip roots, and greens, as well as spicy chorizo and smoked ham—on the table. They hurriedly served two half-full ladles on our plates, and this—just this—along with the slices of bread on the table, was intended to fill our empty bellies and hearts. Even the gift of lingering conversation was denied because there were so many others in line waiting to come in.

As we all silently marched outside and left the soup kitchen behind, life felt to me like such an overwhelmingly sad thing. I hadn't expected for the charitable meal to fill me with such regrets. I hadn't expected to feel as if I no longer belonged anyplace. I hadn't expected to feel as I felt. I hadn't expected to miss my old life or be consumed with laments. I hadn't expected to hate myself for running with Mother after Valentín, to a shiny new life in Spain that I knew nothing about. I hated my weakness for not fighting to stay in Cuba with Nenico and Antonio at their farm.

PREJUDICE

I was sure that finding a job would be a simple task. I believed all that I had been told about the purity of my Spanish bloodline. Besides, my skin was fair rather than dark, and I knew that was an important thing. I had taught myself to speak in a clear manner that was nothing like that of Mother's or Father's or those at the farm. I felt confident in my ability to impress everyone. After all, despite the dark thoughts that lurked in my head, I sought to greet the world with a charming compliment.

But the Madrid I walked into as I looked for work that early spring was nothing like I expected it to be. No matter where I went to look for a job, they all recoiled over the soulful roundness of my voice. To them, it sounded like Andalusian *gitano* speech.

To me, that was a good thing because Benita, Abuela, Father, and I were gypsies by blood, and I was proud of my pedigree. I could not explain their contempt. I didn't understand until Doña Catalina heard my frustration and explained that gypsies were a people forced to live at the edges of Spain's restrictive caste. She explained that gypsies were seen as devious thieves.

Then I understood the angry men pacing back and forth across from the soup kitchen every day. For if they, too, saw us Cubans as gypsies who were entitled to very few things, why then should we be given free food every day?

Only then did I see that it didn't matter how fair one's skin was, how light one's eyes were, how blond one's hair was, or how unpolluted one's Spanish name was. If one was a Cuban in Spain struggling to survive, if one's matter of dress wasn't elegant and refined, if one lived in the poorest neighborhood of Lavapies, as I did, we were the same as gypsies, to be mistrusted and despised. The situation was that I'd never be able find a job at a department store or a fancy shop.

Never-ending cycles of me starting a new menial job that no others would do followed, only to be let go within a few weeks or less than a day because I hadn't been shown how to perform the work properly, or wasn't given a chance to improve. Days when I was hired as a flower shop delivery boy not knowing how to get to and from my destination. Days of me attempting to become a waiter at a restaurant and unable to juggle the many tables or large trays piled up with plates. The long hours behind the counter of a coffee shop where my share of the day's tips was my only pay.

Staring at my fifteen-year-old face in the mirror, all I saw was my accumulated failures chipping away at my ego and feeding my insecurities. My entire life had been a cycle of victories and catastrophes, brief moments of hopeful prosperity pilfered by despair's grip. I wanted off the carousel. I wanted a calm space to settle my rattling insides. I wanted a quiet place, a real home with my own bedroom and my own bed bathed in sunlight, my stomach full, and books to study so I could somehow dig my way out of the trenches of poverty.

Escape

A brightly lit and colorful Hollywood movie teaming with beautiful, tanned blonds played on the screen of a movie theater near Madrid's Puerta del Sol.

Looking up the steps on either side of the dark rows of the balcony, I could see heads appearing and disappearing through the projector's flickering hazy glow. Bodies darted from row to row as if lured by the endless gasping groans. The dank stench from the frayed carpeting and old red velvet seats was everywhere, and the smell of sex lingered in my nose. In the distance, a swinging door opened and closed every time a shadow came in or out of the dimly lit room on the other side. Anticipation and excitement passed through me as I sat alone in an otherwise empty row.

I didn't move when the dark figure came and sat next to me. Even when his hand reached toward my right thigh, my crotch, I let him go on until he came close enough for me to be repulsed by the acrid odor of low-priced tobacco and the sour smell of cheap alcohol.

I jumped from my seat and rushed away from the stranger, toward the swinging black doors, and a dense cloud of cigarette smoke welcomed me in. Through the fog, I could see that the room was filled with men.

Some were svelte professionals dressed in their elegant business suits and ties. Some of them were round-bodied men wearing their caps and wrinkled laborer coveralls. Many were handsome and young, but others were wretchedly old. Looking at their hands, I could see that many had kept their wedding rings on. The anonymity sharpened my senses and quickened my pulse.

Under cracked and foggy mirrors, a quartet of discolored sinks lined up along the left wall. Past a brief partition, six urinals rose from the floor. Beyond the urinals at the end of the room, three stalls broadcast pleasurable cries from behind their locked doors. Between the gasps and cries, a revolving parade of men rushed out from each stall to escape back into their lives and their world. Then just as fast, that man was replaced by one of the others waiting for their turn.

Some of the men stood in front of the urinals, frozen forward as if pretending they were not there at all, while other men reached from behind until they released their force. Still others with money in their hands approached the beautiful young men congregating along a white-tiled wall.

Purchases completed, some of the young men fell to their knees right there and then, while others followed svelte and toady men alike into the darkness of the theater or into the street and places unknown.

I watched the aloof young men who held the power, and I felt comfortable amongst acts like the acts that I had previously known and performed. Confidently, I sized up the competition and understood the power I could hold.

I wondered then, why I should continue to stand behind the coffee shop counter all day for a meager share of the daily tips when I could easily turn myself into one of those beautiful young men. After all, I knew how to entice men. I had always known what they wanted from me.

From that day forward, I returned to the sex theater on the way home from the soup kitchen lunch, but only when I wanted to stop. Sometimes, I only watched the movie on the screen before going home, and that act alone made me feel in control of my life.

I alone controlled who sat next to me or who I'd follow through the swinging black doors and into the bathroom beyond before falling to my knees. I alone made the decision to follow the tall well-dressed man out of the theater and into a bar for a drink as we bargained for my price.

After my first deal, I negotiated my fee before ever following the men into the hotels that catered to our unique trade—hotels where young men were always welcomed as long as they arrived with a patron who paid. Once there, I devoured the sacrifices that these men were so freely willing to make at the altar of my youth, believing that the offerings laid at my feet were the just sum for a brief taste of my flesh.

How many times did I lie to the men when they asked me my age? I do not know when I became such an expert at knowing the exact age the men wanted me to be.

Lying had become such an easy habit for me that I didn't see how I had saved the biggest lies for myself. I refused to see that it was their money that had the power over me and every other eager young man. I refused to admit that deceit reigned at the hands of these married men who wanted to satisfy their hunger and then retreat to their acceptable professions, children, and wives.

I alone made the decision to ignore Anita's and Mariana's concerns by insisting they were not to question my actions because I was bringing in money every day. I alone turned my life into a manic delusion, convinced that I was special, desired, and loved. And I alone chose to deny that all which remained afterward was loneliness, hurt, and regret.

Instead, I pushed away the dangers and warnings as I left one hotel room and ran into another room with the very next man who paid my price.

Summer, Fall, Winter and into Spring, I didn't eat, bathe, or know how to rest. I traveled the streets one day into the next. I alone built the reputation for being the one young man who would never say no, regardless of the torture or the pain. Nothing I did was sufficiently evil or shameful if it meant having fists full of *pesetas* at the end of every game.

Abyss

I can now remember with clarity the night I met Arturo. It had been a beautiful spring afternoon. Madrid's light had chased away the gray gloom of winter, and I sat in the park, soaking up the healing warmth of the sun, as I had done so many times at the farm. The spirit of respite had kissed my weary eyelids, granting me the gift of sleep, which had eluded me for countless nights. My mind was clearer than it had been in days. So what if the sleep had been induced after one of Mother's yellow pills?

At first, I hated that the pills made me feel as if I had never been alive. Yet as the numbness cleared, contentment settled in and hushed the anxious thoughts spinning wild and fast in my head. What a miraculous gift, the little yellow pill that allowed me to sleep and left me believing I was safe and calm. I felt energized as I prepared to go out and roam. I was ready to take on the world.

The city's nightlife ritually started late and ran until the early morning light broke over the rooftops, and the domed cathedrals, through the colonnades and the markets, and peeking over the skyscrapers to brush the avenues in a golden glow. People had worked and studied all week, and by each Friday evening they were ready to indulge and connect. These were the best nights to cruise the city's bars and parks in search of eager, wealthy men.

These rich men were not the married men who frequented the movie theaters or bars during the daytime. These were the men with plenty of money who were able to buy whomever they liked. These were the men we young men were eager to trap. This was the grand prize: a man who fell for our charms and kept returning to us with his money and gifts.

It was by being with them that I learned what to say and how to act, which they rewarded by showing me off to their friends. By studying how they interacted with one another, I learned how to fake interest over the least interesting thing that they said. I already knew about wines, and which knife, and which fork, and which spoon to use with what course. By watching other more experienced young men, I'd learned how to lean forward and seductively ask for a light while holding back their hand as I blew out the flickering match. It was so easy for me to lie and pretend because I felt nothing for these men. I was doing my job. A job I enjoyed. A job that brought money and security into our home. But a job, nonetheless.

It was a typical tapas bar, long and narrow, with just a few small tables and chairs up front. To the right, a short shelf ran the full length of the wall with old Matador posters and photographs hanging above. The bar itself ran along the left side, behind long glass cases lined with heaping dishes of bite-sized delights. I loved the ritual of pointing at the bites I wanted and seeing them placed on my plate, which I balanced on top of my glass as I moved away from the bar.

I always played the same game, standing at the door of a bar to scope out the room before deciding whether to go in or simply move on. I was an expert and could judge with a single glance.

Arturo stood toward the front of the bar, holding a glass of sherry in his ringless, well-manicured hand. His light-gray suit had been immaculately tailored, as if deliberately fashioned to heighten his aristocratic elegance. His smoothly polished skin was rosy rather than tan, and I understood that he had never worked as a laborer a single day of his life. He glowed in the diffused light, making it impossible for me to know how old he was. I imagined that he was thirty-five. As I got close to him, I noticed that he was more than a head taller than me.

His face was framed in honey soft waves and brightened by his olive gemstone eyes. His lips were thin, and he spoke so effortlessly that I quickly fell into a trance. The scent he wore was an intoxicating blend of citrus, spices, and myrrh, and through the sweet cloud from his American cigarette, the consumed alcohol, and his cologne, I felt certain there was great kindness in his heart.

Then, just like that, instead of making him fall for me, I was the one who fell for his charm. I was giddy and fully aroused by the time we walked out the bar. Washed in infatuation, everything around was beautiful. My head was light, and my soul was smiling as we slid into the back of the taxicab, laughing at something amusing he said. I despaired over the fact that I'd allowed myself to become the prey. I was no longer in control. A bit inebriated, it was easy to push the nagging thought away.

I thought it was a delightful room. Its carved wall panels, elaborate headboard, the gilded desk by the window, and the emerald brocade upholstery on the oversized bergère next to the desk seemed quite sophisticated to me. It was as if I had walked into a charming old French salon I'd seen in a film.

Wild fantasies ran through my mind as we franticly kissed, caressed, and undressed. It was then that my senses were heightened by the smell and taste of his flesh, because Arturo smelled and tasted of Sebastián.

Reliving my moments with Sebastián, I performed every act that he had performed that day on my bed. But I didn't rest as he had—rather, I—begged for more, and then even more. I rode the waves of pleasure all night, completely lost in my lust until all my memories of Sebastián's scent and taste had faded away. I'd found a new man to love.

Arturo was staring out the window when I woke. As he turned to look at me, his face was sallow, and it no longer glowed as it had the previous night. Deep creases traveled down the sides of his mouth, and his swollen eyes made him seem gaunt.

I wanted to move toward him, but froze when I saw the look in his eyes. We stood in deafening silence, him dressed in a silk paisley robe by the window, and me naked in the middle of the room. We stood facing one another for a lifetime, until he walked over to me and crushed a fistful of *pesetas* against my chest.

"*¡Anoche fue anoche pero ahora todo se acabó!*" The message was clear: the previous night was in the past, and there would be nothing more.

My heart pierced by rejection, it bled, flooding my body with remorse. For me, that night had been different than all my other nights from my past, and I wanted so much more from him than his money or just another wild ride.

I'd have followed him wherever he asked me to go. If he had asked for me to walk away from my life and follow him, I'd have forgotten everything and everyone without remorse. But he didn't ask, and so, like an undertaker preparing a corpse, I dressed. In silence, I gathered the wrinkled bills from the floor, pushed them deep down into the pocket of my pants, and held onto them. I wanted to hold onto the only part of him I was able to hold. I hesitated to leave the room.

Perhaps he didn't understand that I liked him. Maybe he thought I was like the others, but I wasn't. Honestly, I wasn't.

Abruptly, he grabbed me by the arm, flung me out into the hallway, and slammed the door at my back, just as Padre Felipe had done after my honest confession when I was ten.

My dignity stripped, my heart squeezed dry of the joy I'd so briefly known, I rode the metro home as a hollow survivor of my trade. Sinking into my seat, I tried to make myself as small as possible, an invisible apparition. Repeatedly, I ran both hands through my hair, hopelessly trying to straighten its unruly curls. I stared down at my no longer shining brown shoes in an excuse not to look at anyone because I was sure I'd be met with disapproving stares and glances ripe with disgust. The women from church would be pointing their fans at me, arching their brows, and rolling their eyes in contempt.

Anxiety quickened its pulse as I started down Mesón de Paredes, and it quadrupled when I stopped to look in the window of the store where I liked to shop—the same grocer where I'd gleefully purchased the luscious red apple and mouth-watering piece of yellow cheese on my first day in Spain. The day full of promise, and when I felt so alive.

The sunlight streaked across my face, my image in the glass. I stared at my young reflection, stoic with disappointment like Father's. A glint of light from the shiny chrome of a passing car sliced through my reflection, momentarily blinding me. Blinking to focus, I was startled by the face staring back at me. Mother! It was Mother's eyes. It was Mother's face. My breath caught in my throat, and I froze.

Mad! Mad! I was as mad as Mother. I'd flipped over a man, as she had. A man I'd assumed couldn't resist my charms. A man who never once thought about loving me. I hated my foolish delusion.

I wrapped my arms around myself as tightly as I could, attempting to muffle the pronounced pounding of my wounded heart. I scurried down the middle of the street, refusing to acknowledge the prostitutes standing on the sidewalk laughing at me. I was not them. I was not like them. All I had ever wanted was to be loved. I'd become one of those mad Italian women from the black and white films I'd once laughed at.

I saw no one as I walked up the three flights of stairs to the apartment's black door. Standing in the foyer, I could hear Mother in her room behind her locked door, but said nothing to her. She was the last person I wanted to face. She was the last person from whom I wanted to accept any kindness or love. As if she would have any to offer. Foolish thought. Foolish me.

I heard no one as I continued down the long hall until I reached my room. Habitually, I clicked on the lamp. It felt as if I was lost inside a tunnel with only the flicker of a small candle to light up my path.

I gazed at the ceiling above and imagined it to be the azure skies of my homeland. I raised my empty arms to the heavens, begging for God to fill them with a bounty of happy memories I could hold close to my heart—the happy memories of a verdant Cuban countryside.

My heart cried out for Abuela's rosewater scent and dancing kerosene lamps. It cried for Tía Dulce and her comforting hands. It cried for Papá and Mamá. It cried for my happy days at the farm. But God had abandoned me, and I stood all alone in a life I couldn't understand.

I brought a glass of water into my room and locked the door from the inside. I sat on the cot, gripping Mother's bottle of round yellow pills in my hand. After swallowing the pills and emptying the glass, I switched off the insignificant lamp, laid down, and closed my eyes.

REQUIEM

I awoke in total darkness, unable to see my hand in front of me. The dead silence overwhelming, I strained to hear the slightest sound as I wrestled with a half-dream state of bewilderment. I shook my head. Where was I? Disjointed thoughts flashed in the dark. I tried to swallow, but my throat was raw, and my mouth dry. I slowly stretched my legs and my arms, ran my fingers over my face, and rubbed my eyes. I reeked of cigarette smoke, alcohol, and sex, and the piercing springs of the folding cot stabbing me in the back was evidence I was still alive.

Recovering my senses some more, I clicked the lamp on and sat up, a little too fast, my head in a swirl. Holding tight to my cot, I sat still until the spinning ceased. I was back, trapped in the same four-walled pantry. Checking my watch, I noted the time: 3:49.

Parched, I held the glass to my lips, only to thrust my eager tongue into dry air. My bladder near bursting, I reached for the door.

The apartment was pitch black as I ran my hand over the wall to the bathroom. I'd slept the day away. But how? There must have been people in the house during the day. Had Mother not heard me come in? She must have heard me lock the door. The day had passed and no one, not one single soul, had knocked on my door to check on me.

Damn them! Nobody cared, and so I wouldn't care about them. I was hungry and parched, and I didn't care if I ever saw any of them again. They were all like Mother—selfish, self-centered, and incapable of caring for anyone. Incapable of truly loving someone other than themselves.

Back in my room, I sat on the bed and a sharp pain shot through me. Frightened, I checked myself for blood. Thank God. Nothing. A throbbing that soon, with rest, would stop. Accidentally stubbing my toe on the crate, I cursed the hideous room, and my hideous life, and the horrible Mother who'd dragged me across the world, to be with a man. Someone who had dumped her because she was not able to give birth again.

Mechanically, I laid down on my side, facing the wall, and curled into a ball, covering my eyes with my hand. Wallowing in a misguided rage, I tossed and turned, unable to fall back to sleep. *Please, God! Please! Let me sleep. Let me sleep! Please, God. Let my tears wash the pain away. Please, God. Let me live!*

I hadn't cried since when I was ten years old and Padre Felipe had tossed me out of the church's office door. Too many times I had suppressed the tears, thinking that it would toughen me up, make me a man like Father. Be just like Father. Little had he known that I saw him cry. I'd seen him paralyzed by life and Mother, and crushed by the responsibility he felt for loving me.

But the phantoms I'd refused to acknowledge for most of my life, the demons I could no longer push away, were not finished with me. On by one, they slid under the door, poking, and prodding me, pinching my flesh. I pulled the covers over my head, but they were insistent and tugged on the blanket's hem.

Powerless to stop them, I tossed the covers off. Their hot breath on my bare skin, I convulsed. Anxiety gripped my arms, legs, and hands. I shivered in a cold sweat. I felt a new razor-sharp cut every time a grotesque ghost leapt from my bed and paraded itself in front of me, it only moving aside to allow the next ghost to take center stage and dance its dance. One after one, they held my body down and insisted I watch.

That was the moment when they introduced themselves by their name: Madness, Neglect, Rape. Again and again, they laughed, repeatedly chanting their names.

I wrapped the pillow around my head, trying to hide, but they yanked it away and stamped on it and continued to dance. In a suffocating grip, they held tightly onto me, gnawing at my heart, making sure I felt every bite. I begged them to stop, but they were joyously lost in the thrill of their violent act.

I felt as though a hole had been dug into my chest and my soul had been butchered. Nevertheless, I'd stared at madness, neglect, and rape and survived the phantoms of my past.

Only then, once I saw them for who and what they were, after surviving all their inflicted pain and shame, after seeing that I was still alive, was I able to cry.

REPRIEVE

O n the street, strangers went about their day as I stood unnoticed at the building's threshold. From her threshold, the redheaded prostitute blew a kiss at me, as she did whenever she saw me. I'd always ignore her in the past, but this time I pretended to catch it. Astonishing both myself and her, I smiled and she laughed.

I wanted to be kind. I no longer wished to look at her with disgust, I understood. After all, weren't we the same? I felt as clean as the day when the rains washed the town and Abuela's house because I saw forgiveness in my heart.

The perimeters inside the church were quite dark, contrasting greatly to the magnificent dome at its center bursting with light. I slid into a pew and took a moment to collect myself, allowing the street noise in my head to fade from my mind. Only a few blocks away, I'd passed the peasant church many times, joining the crowds to watch the procession of their saint. I wasn't sure why I'd entered, but I was glad I was there. I wanted to rest.

Rhythmically chanting just a few pews ahead, an old woman reached out to God. I hadn't noticed her at first, all dressed in black, her small round figure melting into the darkness. Maybe I, too, wanted to reach out to God, to forgive him for having abandoned me. Had he forgiven me?

Inhaling deeply, I filled my lungs as if I were learning how to breathe for the first time. With each breath, expanding calmness shrouding me until all I heard was the old widow's spellbinding chant, and all I saw was the light at the center of the church. Each breath propelled me closer to the vaulted ceiling above, her prayer on my lips: *"Padre nuestro que estás en el cielo..."* Our Father, who art in heaven...

The terrazzo floor below, the heavy columns supporting the dome, the dark walls spiced with mystery, the sacred side chapels, the glittering gilded altar, the pagan statuaries, the strong scent of white lilies, the faint aroma of the burning candles in their offertory stands, my anger, my pain—only the echoed prayers and the light existed for me.

A New Door

"Joaquín," he said with a sincere smile as he unfolded the towel rolled under his arm and sat next to me.

The sloping grassy incline I'd selected was serene in the cool of the shady tree protecting us from the insistent sun on that early summer day. From that vantage point, one could easily see and hear the crowd enjoying themselves around the municipal pool.

"Martín," I replied. He said, "*Madrileño.*" Without thinking, I said, "*Habanero,*" as if we both had tapped into some familiar and equally inherited cultural decree driving us to search for a common place for the conversation to start.

He was slight and shorter than me, no more than five-foot-five. Looking directly at him, I noticed first the long dark lashes surrounding brilliantly blue eyes. Then I noticed his gentle black curls. Seeing that I was staring at him, he lifted the arch of his brows and mischievously laughed, almost as if fully conscious that this action would make his eyes appear bigger still. He smiled at me with his eyes, and I found myself feeling self-conscious as I brought down my own gaze.

His face had a certain familiarity that I wasn't able to place. It was a handsome face. His jaw was strong but without the exaggerated lines of a Hapsburg. His lips were full, and his smile was honest and bright. He had an average straight nose with lion nostrils flanked by widespread cheekbones. I thought that his curls perfectly framed the face. His skin was smooth, unsoiled, and it glowed in the summer's daylight. The cadence in his voice spoke of his education and echoed the music in his eyes. He wore brown leather sandals displaying beautiful feet, tan pants, and a light cotton shirt.

We spoke of nothing significant for a brief time, but then the conversation continued at an increasingly relaxing stride. I told him about me, where I was from, how long I had been living in Spain. I told him that I worked since that spring at a hotel, catering to well-traveled tourists near Paseo de la Castellana, and heard about the pool from some of the people at work. It had been a long ride from the hotel to an unknown part of the city, and I had no idea where I was. I knew that the bus drove around the popular bull fighting arena just before I got off and walked to the municipal park, and I figured I could easily trace my way back.

"*Un camarero,*" I said in an almost inaudible voice, as to hide my embarrassment. But his response was positive, and he joked about the tourists' willingness to give generous tips to the serving staff. "*Entonces buenas propinas ¿No? Sí, buenísimas,*" I replied, proudly accepting his sympathetic remarks.

He told me that his family was from Segovia, but that both he and his sister were born and raised in Madrid. When he asked how old I was, I hesitated, not knowing what answer to give. He replied by telling me he was nineteen. I didn't lie, and told him I was sixteen. He then signaled his desire to run into the pool, and I was glad that he'd asked.

Undressing came fast, given that we were both wearing our bathing suits under our pants. He placed the folded clothes under his towel and looked over to a grandmother watching two toddlers, and asked if she could keep an eye on them for him. She agreed, and I then asked the same with the shortest of smiles, worried about the few *pesetas* in my pocket, which was all the money I had with me that day. Noticing my apprehension, he placed his hand on my shoulder and told me not to worry. "*No te preocupes.*" His action bringing some unexpected relief. I let him walk ahead of me, happy for the opportunity to observe his physique.

I first noticed his solid Spanish legs—those legs that some Cubans called *patas gallegas* to describe men's legs that are shapely from their knees down to their ankles. They were the same legs that I had always lusted after during my childhood trips to the beach, and were quite a contrast from my thin ankles and laborer calves. Our chests and body hair were proportionally matched.

Joaquín found an open spot and quickly jumped in the pool. In an unplanned urge to show off, I ran up the tall ladder to bounce off the diving board. We tried to swim, but the pool was crowded, so we soon decided to leave.

With late afternoon approaching, we looked at each other without speaking a word, and in synchrony got dressed, folded our towels, and started to walk.

He said he had his car with him, and asked if I wanted a ride. I said yes, but feeling ashamed of letting him see me get out in front of the prostitute's door, I told him to drop me off at Puerta del Sol.

The ride down the beautiful broad and unfamiliar avenues felt like a perfect ending to a perfect afternoon. Joaquín seemed quite content to drive in silence as I looked out of my window, leaning forward to better see what was ahead, or turned back to catch one last glance of the scenery. Riding in his car felt as magical as my first *guaguita* ride had felt. Every time he smiled at me, the child in me rejoiced, and I felt as if my spirit was free.

As we approached the Cibeles fountain, the jubilant pleasure of being in recognized territory made me feel safe, and I gazed at him with enormous eyes. He grinned and gently mussed my hair between gear shifts.

The tiny black sedan continued down El Paseo del Prado and past the Neptuno fountain before turning. Unexpectedly, he asked if I wanted to meet him at El Retiro park the next day. Elated, I agreed, and I could see he was pleased that I had.

We were near the busy square of Puerta del Sol, in the heart of the city, when he quickly pulled over to drop me off. Leaning near, he gently kissed my cheek and reminded me that we were meeting the next day. Puzzled as to how I should respond, I held his hand for an instant, before quickly getting out of the car. For that brief lightheaded moment, my life once again had become a joyful whisper in time.

I stood on the sidewalk and waved as he drove away, overcome by the same freedom and contentment that I had only felt on my own at the farm. I just stood there inhaling my delight at the dawning realization that such emotion could be experienced with someone of my own age at my side.

Deliberately, I slowed my pace as I walked across the square and down the crowded streets. I was in no hurry to get home. What was waiting there for me? I didn't want to walk down Mesón de Paredes, only to lock myself inside my windowless pantry bedroom.

In a haze, I had lost track of where I was and stopped to gain my bearing, only to see that Tirso de Molina was across the street.

With my heart filled with joy, I darted through the traffic to walk into the small triangular park, and sat under a tree to watch the people around me.

The cloudless day had turned into a starry night above. I made no effort to get up and go.

Honesty

Coming up the stairs of the metro station, I thought that my heart would explode. What if Joaquín wasn't there waiting for me?

I took the stairs two steps at a time, and I was breathless by the time I got to the top. When I looked around, only to see that he wasn't there, my heart dropped. I stood motionless for what felt like an eternity.

The fear that I was about to faint vanished the second I felt someone from behind wrap their arms around my waist before spinning me quite fast. I didn't lose my footing because Joaquín held me tight while he laughed.

Freeing myself from his hold, I grabbed him by the shoulders and shook him gently for a brief moment, and he grinned. Then, reaching under his arms, I pulled him close to me and burst into laughter.

"*¿Listo?*"

"*Claro*," I replied, more than ready for our adventure to start.

Joaquín took the lead, walking down to the next corner and crossing the busy road. Further to our right, La Puerta de Alcalá held court. Side by side, we walked through the imposing iron gates and into the park.

The broad expanse ahead led to a well-manicured path lined with trees and anchored by flower beds. At the end of the path, a large rotunda containing a whimsical fountain with dolphin-riding cherubs seemed happy to greet us. To the right, an enormous body of water awaited. A striking monument stood at the highest point on the opposite side of the lake and was flanked by a crescent-shaped colonnade.

We talked little as we walked, but the silence didn't feel awkward. It seemed that he was eager find a quiet place where we could talk. I was happy to follow where he led.

Down the isolated, narrow lane that ran along the back of the arcade, we settled on a simple stone bench. Quiet and still, it was a lovely spot where we could relax. In the stillness, only the whisper of the rustling leaves overhead broke through the silence, and it felt as if the cooling breeze had cradled me in its arms.

I do not know how long I was lost in my thoughts, or at what point I discovered that I no longer cared about which mask covered my face. I fell in love with the freedom I felt while sitting next to him. Still, I wondered if I should dare to trust him—or myself.

The breath of an angel caressed my face and brought me back to the bench and to Joaquín. Why not that? God's light had welcomed us when we entered the park. It had winked at us through the trees along the promenade. Its rainbow had leapt off the fountain's playful outbursts. It had reflected against the waves of the lake. Certainly, a benevolent angel had been walking with us all the time.

Slowly and ever so softly, Joaquín spoke about attending the university during the week, and his hope of becoming a doctor someday. He spoke about his family, who'd lived abroad for a time, and about his father's career at an important international bank.

I didn't ask where they lived because I didn't care to hear about his marvelous life. I felt out of place and outclassed. I listened and smiled, but inside, panic gripped me. None of my training at the hands of men had prepared me for this. I didn't want to use the same old tricks on him. I wanted to be me, but I didn't really know who that was. So I listened and smiled tenderly at him as he shared the story of his life with me.

Unexpectedly, he asked about me. He asked about my life, my hopes. He asked about my dreams. But what hopes did I have anymore? I didn't know how to explain to him that for so long, my only hope had been to survive. In terror, I dusted off the same old well-rehearsed tired act.

Within just one breath, I talked about Abuelito Agustín, and about the acres of land. I talked about La Finca, and about its indoor plumbing and the imported tile floors throughout the whole house. I talked about the river valley where the family cattle roamed. I talked about the family's successful businesses and being one of the respected families on the block. I talked about the government taking away the farm. This time, I didn't stop then, as I had always done in the past. Instead, I took an enormous breath, wiped the tears only I could see from my eyes, and in another single breath, continued to speak.

I talked about Valentín's betrayal and Mother's breakdown afterward. I talked about her wanting to return to Cuba to be at her mother's dying bedside. I talked about me never wanting to return to Cuba again. I talked about me wanting to remain in Spain, but that I didn't know how do that. Then I stopped in fear, shame, and in pain.

Quiet once again, my heart was filled with pride for not having reached out for a lie. Pride in knowing that I hadn't resorted to a delusional fantasy. Had I gone too far with sharing my life? I prepared myself for our budding relationship to end there and then.

Without hesitation, Joaquín reached over to me, held my face in his hands, and said that he understood. Then he asked once again about my dreams and the things that I wanted from life.

I became quiet once again for a time, until with great hesitation, I spoke about my ambitions for a better life, admitting I didn't really know how to achieve such a goal. Secretly, I knew that any place where I felt safe and cared for would qualify as a much better life.

I spoke about my heritage and the drive that had brought my ancestors to Cuba, and as if needing to assure myself more than him, I spoke of me having inherited that drive. I spoke about my ability to remember things without ever writing them down in class. I told him that all I wanted form life was a chance, as silly as all that seemed at the time. When the moment came for me to be honest with him, asking life for a chance seemed like the perfect thing for me to ask.

He took a few seconds to speak, as if searching for the right response. When he did, he assured me that he understood, and that he admired me for being as driven as him. I couldn't have hoped for a better reply.

As we journeyed back, Joaquín kept nudging me and bumping into me. I faked irritation, but my smile clearly showed him how happy I was. Maybe being honest had been the right role for me to play this one time, and I felt relieved in believing that the chance of getting to know him hadn't died, after all. I felt the new pleasure of having been honest for once.

We crossed the street near the grand Alcalá arch, and headed back toward the metro entrance and stopped in front of the café. Plopping down in a chair, he pulled me down to next to him and asked me what I wanted to drink. I ordered a Fanta orange soda—my favorite. We lingered over our drinks and spoke about the beauty of the park and the wonderful time we'd both had.

Despite the happy events of the day, so much of me remained fearful that I'd done something wrong in sharing my life with Joaquín. I thought him a young, inexperienced nineteen-year-old, especially since he'd lived a charmingly beautiful life.

Before getting up, he leaned over and whispered in my ear, saying he wanted to take me out on the town the next Friday night. I felt relieved.

We slowly walked up to the same metro stop where we'd met earlier that day, and just as before, we hugged, giggled, and laughed.

I heard a flirtatious whistle as I descended the stone steps and felt flattered when I looked back to see him standing there, a happy smile on his face, and waving his goodbyes.

ROUTINE

I wanted to be at my best for my next date with Joaquín, but instead I started the week completely overwhelmed with angst.

Our two earlier meetings felt to me as a dream which brought with it the same peaceful feelings that I had felt at Abuela's house as I danced with the flames from the kerosene lamps. Perhaps she was the benevolent angel who'd gently kissed my face in the park.

But what about my own demons and drives? I had been good since the day I heard the chanting woman in church and communed with the light. Even when I felt the urge, I hadn't returned to the bathrooms or trolled the streets or the bars at night. Still, the thirst remained, despite my fears about falling into another yellow-pill demon dance, certain that I wouldn't survive the next time.

I wanted to be good. I didn't want any harm to come to Joaquín. I worried about what would happen if I ran into any of the men from my past when I was out with him. What if they made it clear that they knew who I was? How would Joaquín react to such news?

Thankfully, I had my rituals at work to keep me occupied, and I welcomed the breakfast to late-afternoon shift. I didn't even mind when I was asked to help with the elaborate dinner setup.

I liked working to make the guests think their evening meal experience was something grand. After all, the food served at the hotel was nothing more than well-presented peasant food. I relished the thought that the mostly American, Dutch, and German tourists enjoyed the same *caldo gallego* that sustained so many Cubans at the soup kitchen.

Bright-white and heavily starched linen tablecloths were unfolded and laid out first, followed by the precise placing of deep cream-colored plates perfectly trimmed with a thin gold band. Matching napkins, buffed silverware, and spotless stemware completed the setup. A tall, thin-cut glass vase with fresh carnations and a single sprig of wispy fern adorned the table, while a votive candle came last.

I welcomed the assembly line, performing the tasks one after one, placing a cloth on each of the tables before coming back with a stack of plates in my arms, taking the heavy silverware tray from one table to the next, and buffing the utensils separately before placing them in their own assigned spot—these ritualized tasks helped me to numb the fears in my heart.

By that Friday afternoon, at the end of my workday, exhausted from the long hours, I had convinced myself that I could easily conquer whatever happened that night.

Release

My world had been an unending parade through dark theaters, dingy bathrooms, smoky bars, and unmade beds. But the world that Joaquín shared with me that night was clean, brightly lit, and inhabited by sophisticated young people who welcomed me with open arms. Still, I feared that my own peasant bloodline would show, and they'd stop wanting me in their lives.

I knew how to hide behind my looks and my gift for drawing people in. I had studied and listened, and could talk about things in a manner that made me seem older than I actually was. I knew I could hide behind my façade. And so, cloaked in my tools and tricks, we hopped from one tapas bar to the next, meeting his friends at each stop.

It was after eleven when we approached a table where a jubilant group was engaged in frantic debate. I was startled when one of the young women from the group jumped up and kissed and hugged me before Joaquín introduced us. She was handsome more than beautiful, and her gregarious demeanor gave her a certain grace. Her straight auburn hair, parted in the middle, draped long past her shoulders and onto the round collar of her close-fitting white lace top. She wore a short brown and red plaid skirt, which matched the colors of her chunky Mary Janes.

"*Mi hermana Pilar,*" Joaquín said with a sense of familial pride as he introduced me to his sister. And just like that, she welcomed me into her life. I felt safe next to Pilar and Joaquín. I felt loved. I felt clean and reborn.

COMMUNION

I didn't know where I was, but that didn't matter. I was with Joaquín, and he was the one person I knew I could trust. All around us, tall, handsome buildings anchored sidewalks and rows of trees.

He had been polite—sweet, even—when asking if I'd like to spend the night with him. He bashfully said that his heart wished for nothing else, as we walked to his car.

I felt special because this was the first time I'd ever been asked. I felt respected, at last.

The apartment was small, but the boxy avocado sofa with the tangerine and lemon chairs were artfully placed. "*El piso de mis tíos*," Joaquin said, explaining that it belonged to his aunt and uncle who only visited Madrid from time to time.

That night, I allowed myself to be led by Joaquín. I wanted to be everything that he wanted me to be. I reacted to his touch and caress as if it had been my very first time. I relaxed and let his emotions nurture me, and returned his affections without hesitation or regrets.

We drank the wine and ate the bread until both of our souls melded into one flesh, and we fell asleep in each other's arms.

Normal

When I woke up, I was alone in bed. I called out to Joaquín, but there was no reply. I put my underpants on and walked the length of the apartment, but I was there alone. I sat on the avocado sofa in a panic, not knowing what I should do. I didn't know if I should wait, or if I should get dressed and go. I sat there frozen in place, tears flowing from my eyes. I sat there until the door opened and Joaquín walked in with hot chocolate and churros.

Seeing me tremble, he sat next to me, took my face in his hands, and kissed my forehead, my eyes, my lips, and then I knew that I'd be safe as long as he was with me. I accepted his affection, even though the nagging guilt tugged on my heart. I knew that I needed to tell him who I really was and what I'd been.

I tried to be honest with him, but he stopped me and assured me that the past didn't matter to him. *"El pasado ya no importa. Mi ángel. Mi amor."*

Suddenly, my world changed. He'd called me his angel, his love, and the emotions I had bottled up, bubbled up because he loved me, not for my looks or the sex, but because he felt the love that I felt for him. I knew it. In my heart, I was certain of it.

From that day forward, my life became days of work, and evenings of phone conversations with Joaquín. Friday evenings out with friends, and nights together in our happy borrowed flat. Saturday mornings were for hot chocolate and churros, followed by long walks through whatever park we fancied. We'd visit El Prado Museum to admire the art, or take journeys though the rugged countryside. In his car, drives to Toledo, and walks down its impossibly narrow streets. Visits to El Escorial, the historical home of the king. I felt delightfully ordinary for the very first time in my life.

A Perfect Bowl

I felt anxious as I walked up the steep metro steps to join Joaquín. Me meeting Don Pepe and Doña Lucia was important to him. Being allowed to bring his first love home was such a wondrous thing. I wanted to appear undamaged for his sake.

For weeks, he'd behaved like an excited child as he planned how to break the news to his parents about him and me. Night and day, I worried that I'd disappoint them, him, and myself. I fretted that they'd never accept me. Never fall in love with me.

After greeting me as affectionately, as he'd always done, Joaquín held onto my arm as we began walking down the gorgeous street where he lived. This common gesture between friends had been so unusual for me. In Cuba, it wasn't possible for males to be seen anywhere arm-in-arm. But in Madrid, this was second nature for men and women alike. I liked how it made me feel. I liked walking down the street with him, my arm in his.

I was relieved when Pilar opened the door and greeted me with a hug and a kiss. I'd worried so much about his father opening the door and looking me up and down with disapproval. Instead, Joaquín, Pilar, and I walked together into the living room. Their parents were nowhere to be seen.

I had expected the low-ceiling room to be filled with similar furniture as the apartment that Joaquín and I had made our home. Instead, it was furnished with dark, unmatched wooden antiques. The sofa and chairs were upholstered in a threadbare brocade. Lumpy pillows were tossed about. Landscape and portrait paintings hung on nearly every wall, as if they had been removed from a museum's walls. As far as I could see, the newest pieces in the room were the two large, round ceramic lamps with enormous shades, like those that had been popular when I was a kid. The disorder, the lack of pretense, made me feel at ease.

Doña Lucia walked in first, and she was nothing like the sophisticated lady with flawless makeup and hair that I had imagined her to be. Rather, she was short, round, and jolly. Her frizzy auburn hair was like Mamá's hair on a humid summer day. I hadn't expected her to greet me with a kiss, but this small gesture was all I needed to feel at ease and ready for Don Pepe just then entering the room.

My expectations of him had been correct as I studied his long face, thinning hairline, and calm stance. But most important of all, he greeted me with such a kind and respectful manner that I felt instantly at home in their house.

Just like with every other home that held some meaning for me, the meal of hearty chorizo, potatoes, leeks, and white bean soup followed by ham, sausages, hard cheeses, and strong bread echoed the comfort I felt. But this meal reserved its magical gift for the end, when Doña Lucia brought out a dessert with layers of yellow cake and custard which had been drenched in a citrusy syrup and covered in marzipan.

As I walked with Joaquín back to my metro stop, he couldn't hide his euphoria because he was so pleased at how well the evening had gone, and so proud of me. It was then that he told me of his plans to ask Don Pepe to somehow sponsor Mother and me so that we could stay in Spain and cancel our plans to move to the States.

I knew how futile such a request would be. I couldn't imagine a family who'd be willing to accept such a burden— being responsible for a boy of sixteen, and a woman they'd never met. Besides, Mother's pride would never allow her to agree to such a thing. Furthermore, she knew nothing about my life with Joaquín. Knowledge of such a life would surely be devastating news.

No. As much as I wished for such a thing, I knew that it was never to be. I didn't want to crush his hope, so I simply encouraged him to follow his dream.

TRIBUTE

Doña Catalina liked to talk about the beauty of her youth, but to me she was simply an old woman who wore her hair in out-of-fashion tight waves. As for her short, wide frame, I often wondered how she remained upright on such petite feet as hers. They were so plump, the flesh spilled over the sides of her open-toed shoes. This may have been the reason her body waddled when she walked. Nonetheless, she was comical rather than sad, and it was impossible to remain unhappy when she was around.

Her voice was particularly unique because it mimicked the sounds she made by constantly opening and closing her Spanish fan. She often started a sentence with a deep breath, a cooling stroke, and a cry—¡Ay, mi corazón!—because she liked to make sure we all knew about her palpitations, conveniently ignoring the fact that we also saw her run up and down the stairs without uttering a single complaint.

Her energy was endless, beyond what anyone expected from someone her age. And as if to prove the point, she liked to be active for hours on end. If her hands were not busy with her fan, then they were busy knitting sweaters and socks. In fact, her floral canvas bag, stuffed with needles and wool, was always by her side.

That is how I remember her best: sitting in a corner of the dining room filled with the friends she'd collected, all waiting to have their hair set and their nails polished. It was a curious thing how she held the one pinky up just so for the wool coil, from inside the bag, to rest on as she knitted it into the piece she was working on.

For many weeks, La Doña had stayed away throughout Mother's cries. But then came that one bright morning when she seemed to have had enough. She opened the door to Mother's room, knitting bag in hand, and closed it behind her.

She repeated the same routine every day, until Mother walked into the dining room on her way to the shower, behaving as if all her dramatics had never happened. After closing the bathroom door shut, Mother sang as if she were the happiest person in the world.

Anita, Mariana, and I flocked to Doña Catalina's side as she stood at the room's threshold. She said nothing, and we held our breath while her shoes clickety-clacked across the room. Only then, after making herself comfortable on her chair, did she speak at last: "*Mira, que escuché todas las torturas de su vida. La escuché hasta que no tuvo nada que decir.*" Look, she told us, I heard all the tortures of her life. I listened to her until she hadn't a thing to say. Then Doña Catalina ended with the sigh of a person who knew she had accomplished an impossible task. But she wasn't finished. After a long pause, she spoke again: "*Es que yo quiero mucho a esa niña.*" It is that I love that girl very much, she explained.

I was taken aback by her words. I wasn't ready to render Mother blameless when it came to the failures of my life. After all, had she not been the one person who took over my pain, time and again? She was the one who'd kept me away from Nenico, Antonio, and my inheritance of the farm. She was the one who refused to show me compassion after my shame at the laboring camp. No, she couldn't possibly be a harmless child who deserved pity, much less my forgiveness.

Yet it was hard to hold my grudge because the person who emerged from Mother's room was someone whose mood was stable and bright. This new person was helpful and kind. Most of all, this new person was affectionate with me and with everyone. And all this was a new experience for me because affection had never been something she knew how to give. I had certainly been kept clean, well-dressed, and fed, but showing affection had never been one of her daily gifts. Despite all her cries and laments, she'd treated me the same way that Mamá had treated her, and I hated her for that. I hated how she'd behaved toward me because she knew personally how such neglect felt. I hated her because she couldn't grant me the affection that I clearly needed.

I didn't know what to do with all the anger and rancor that I'd felt toward her for such a long time. I wasn't ready to trust after so many years of distrust. I couldn't because I was sure this new person wasn't real, but a temporary phantom. I couldn't open my heart to her, only to be disappointed again. So I acted politely toward her, but recoiled whenever she came close to me. I didn't want to be touched—at least, not by her. Perhaps in time my trust would come, but not right there and then. In that instant, my heart held no love for her.

The moment for honesty came one evening when I walked into Mother's room, determined to negotiate. I had planned what I was going to say. I had intended to ease into the conversation, but once sitting at her bedside, I didn't see the need to waste any time with a flowery chat.

"¿Dime por favor, porque tú siempre estabas tan infeliz conmigo? ¿Es que tienes miedo de que yo soy como Nenico?" Tell me please, why were you always so unhappy with me? Are you afraid that I'm like Nenico?

I asked without any warning or preparation. I asked without considering how she would react. I hadn't imagined her entire body becoming rigid. I didn't care that she pulled back and stared at me with panic in her eyes. Rather, I was relieved, as if the avalanche of my hurried words had swept away the awesome weight, at last.

I continued without pause. *"Mira, Margarita. Por claro que yo lo soy pero que también tengo una persona que me ama, tal como Antonio ama a Nenico. Quiero que tú lo conozcas. Quiero que tú conozcas a Joaquín."* Look, Margarita. Of course I am, but I also have a person who loves me, just like Antonio loves Nenico. I want you to meet him. I want you to meet Joaquín.

This time, she didn't pull further back. Instead, her body grew limp as tears flowed from her eyes. I held back all expressions of affection waiting for her to react. I waited in protective stillness until her crying came to a quiet end and she timidly reached for me. Only then did I show my cards, for I was sure I held the winning hand.

"¡Ese es mi precio! Es el precio de entrada para nosotros tratarnos como madre e hijo y no como enemigos. ¿Que tú crees?"

That is my price! I told her. It is the price of entry for us to treat each other as mother and son, and not as enemies. What do you think?

I asked what she thought rather than what she wanted because I knew that to her, these weren't the same thing.

"Bien." Fine, was her only reply, and her answer granted me the permission I needed to give her a gentle, but still distant, hug while placing a nearly forgiving kiss on her cheek. I felt as if all things in life were possible for me.

I'd spent so much energy needing to be noticed, accepted, wanted. Devoted all my labors erecting walls against Mother's manic highs and devastating lows. Wasted so many moments feeling I was responsible for it all. Lived so many endless seconds wanting to be loved. And all at once, I felt the freedom that came from seeing that I had indeed been loved. For when the moment came for Mother to stand against the wall, she chose me as I was—as I had always been.

After a lifetime of hurt, it wasn't much to ask, I realized. And I feared that she had simply given in, as some trapped animals do when they know there is no other recourse.

After all the years of Mamá's disapproving coldness, the years of Father's readiness to run away rather than eagerness to engage, the years of not understanding who or what I was—after all the misguided trusts she had placed on Valentín—perhaps agreeing to meet Joaquín was the greatest show of love she could offer me.

Our lives had been one long corridor where many doors begged to be opened, while never promising a way of return. How many one-way doors had Mother and I separately crossed while feeling sure that we were stepping into a much happier world?

At last, Mother and I had opened the same door.

LAST TEMPTATION

There we all were, gathered in the same light-filled yellow dining room where Doña Catalina had spent so many moments knitting sweaters and socks. We were sitting around the same dining table that had been so familiar to me—the table where the girls and I had held hands while fearing an unknown future. The same table where Anita, Mariana, and Mother worked every day.

There was Mother sitting at one end, as Joaquín sat next to her. In front of us was a Cuban lunch feast of roasted pork, black beans, rice, fried ripe plantains, and all the comforts to make him feel welcomed and loved. And through it all— the meal; the conversation; the jokes; the moments when I placed my head on Joaquín's shoulder, expressing my love; through Anita's and Mariana's outward signs of support; through Doña Catalina's matriarchal expression of delight— Mother sat there, clearly enjoying Joaquín's attention and kindness toward her.

After so many years of me fighting for a world where I fit in, the years of unknowingly fighting Mother to back off and let met me be, none of the drama, trauma, and pain seemed to matter in that moment.

After so many dry years since that summer night at the farm when I stared at the Milky Way as the crickets played their violins and the frogs played their horns, I was once again surrounded by the people I loved.

I should have felt great happiness. I should have felt unending gratification. Yet I felt overwhelmed and missed the familiar monsters that I had lived with daily. They had been my most loyal companions for so long. They had sustained me whenever I'd been left abandoned or unloved.

Having cracked the door for them again, they pushed their way in and pointed out that what was ahead of me was a life of routine and drudgery. A life without any education or profession because I lacked the funds and connections that Joaquín had enjoyed from the day he was born.

Yes, I had him in my life, but they assured me that I wouldn't be enough for him because a hotel waiter could never bring any value to the doctor's life he wanted to build. Easily, they convinced me that it was only a matter of time before I'd be abandoned by him, just as all the men I had loved had abandoned me.

So I told myself that what I wanted was a life where I, too, could live in a great big house surrounded by a manicured green lawn. A life where all my friends were beautiful blondes. A life where I could again tell myself that I was in control of the rich new men attracted to my flesh. A life soothed by the detached physicality that had accompanied me since my bodega day with Fernando when I was eight. I understood such a life.

An avalanche of lies crushed me as I told myself I had cause, because Joaquín's lovemaking had been a peaceful and gentle thing, but that this wasn't enough for me. And these lies clouded my thoughts when I convinced myself that being present in the moment and having to feel every emotion as he did, was terrifying for me. When I told myself that I couldn't stay in Spain with Joaquín, pretending to be happy, because our life was suffocating to me.

It was better to walk away, go on and get ready to move to the States, because I needed to gain an education and connections if I was to ever be famous and rich. Mother's cousins in the States had often written about us moving in with them so that I could return to high school and then attend a city university by taking advantage of the many grants and benefits available to people like me.

I could do that. I could pretend to be innocent all over again. I could find a way to fit in amongst all those unexperienced boys and girls of sixteen. I could pretend to be anything, while leading a clandestine life of promiscuity if it meant I could become all the things I wanted to be.

Joaquín and I had only known each other for a few months, after all. Once I moved to the States, he would see our romance as a fleeting fantasy. He was young and had his family, his friends, his education, and an infinite future ahead of him. I dismissed Joaquín asking me to stay in Spain, as a romantic, childish wish. I was sure that Don Pepe would say that sponsoring Mother and me could never be because she was a stranger, a woman who'd never tried to build a life for herself in Spain. Why take such a job on when failure would be the only pay?

But such dark thoughts seemed out of place right there at the table with everyone celebrating my life with Joaquín. I put them aside and joined in the laugher as Anita amused the crowd by talking about the Galicia donkey ride to her hilltop ancestral home. And I made myself laugh louder still when she told us about her cousin Rosario's arm pits and legs needing a shave.

I knew I could not share my feelings with anyone, because sharing my confusion would have only caused them unimaginable heartache.

Instead, I pulled out one of many masks I hid behind and lied to everyone when Mariana asked me if I was happy having Joaquín sitting right next to me. I said that I was very happy indeed. *"En este momento yo me siento muy feliz."*

I could see that Joaquín didn't understand my coldness, or why I acted so dismissively when we said goodbye before he walked down the metro steps. Did he look back hoping to see a smile on my face? I didn't know. I hadn't waited there until he disappeared from my sight, as I had always done.

I wandered around until I found myself standing in front of the movie theater with the cracked foggy mirrors and the men with money in their hands. I wanted to go in because I felt lost, vulnerable, bruised. I wanted to feel nothing at all. I wanted to be engulfed by the numbness I'd always felt inside that bathroom when surrounded by all the faceless men.

But I resisted and didn't go in. Instead, I stayed there frozen against a wall from across the street as my mind ran away to a zinnia forest of make-believe. Only my eyes stayed to catalog the men coming out and going in.

My body remained frozen in place until a man came over and propositioned me. Then my free-floating spirit was dragged back into my body, and I felt the pain of my burning flesh.

I felt trapped. I felt disgust for the man, for me, for all the things I had been and thought I still wanted to be. I wanted to break free. Unexpected clarity broke through the panic to remind me about Joaquín being such a precious gift to me when I most needed someone like him. How could I ever walk away from him? He was innocent and didn't deserve such betrayal.

What kind of person would I be If I did such a thing? Despite it all, I had always seen myself as good. This was a test, and if I stepped back into that bathroom world, I knew what the consequence for me would be.

What was scarier, I asked myself—living an endless life of forbidden sexual misdeeds and abandonment, or stepping into a love-filled life I wasn't sure I could ever fulfill?

I turned away from the propositioning man and walked the few blocks to Puerta del Sol, down the metro steps.

I crossed the street at La Puerta de Alcalá and entered the park's golden gates. Ahead of me were the same stones under my feet; the same trees, now with leaves not as bright in the October chill; the same fountain, now dormant in front of me; the same lake, now still; the same bench where Joaquín and I once talked and shared each other's dreams.

I sat all alone in the cold with my thoughts, recalling the time when I took the yellow pills, and my moment at that church afterward—the day when Joaquín and I met, the beauty of the life we had built.

I took a slow breath and another breath, followed by even more breaths, each one calmer than the first, bringing the air deeper and deeper into my lungs.

I was fine. I was strong.

ORACLES

The call came right before dawn. *"¿Señorito Martín Cruz? ¿El hijo de la Señora Margarita?"*

The soft-spoken woman, who introduced herself as a nun, confirmed who I was just before asking that I get to the hospital without delay. Mother's surgery hadn't gone well. She then explained that Mother had been taken back to the operating room in the middle of the night to stop the bleeding that would not end.

But what surgery was she talking about? Had Mother not gone away with Doña Catalina to visit a friend?

I recognized the long hallway running along the center of the ward the minute I walked in. And I recognized the same envelope of glossy laurel green paint up to waist level, and the creamy butter paint reaching to the ceiling above. I recognized the row of fans performing their quiet duty in rhythmic accord. I recognized all those things because I once visited the place of my birth when Tía Dulce waited there for her son to be born. This hospital ward in Spain mirrored that place in Cuba I had always tried to forget.

How could I be happy remembering the place where Father had accused Mother of being unfaithful to him? I didn't want to remember the endless fights and accusations that we all had endured. I wanted to run away from Mother and what was just ahead. But the situation demanded that I behave as a dutiful son, even if I had never been such a thing because I didn't know how to treat her tenderly.

Mother seemed like a still child in her sleep, but her bed was like what I had always imagined an open coffin to be. An intravenous bottle was connected to one of her arms, and a bottle of blood was connected to the other arm. Mother and I were all alone.

Was this death? I had never been this close to death. I had brushed Abuela's death aside with my singing and by telling everyone that I was happy for her. But that had been easy to do because I wasn't there at her side. This was different. This felt devastatingly real to me.

I wanted to cross one of my many imaginary doors and never look back again. I wished for Joaquín to be there because he could explain the scene to me. I wanted to place my head on his chest and feel safe, as I always did.

I didn't sit on her bed, choosing to stand instead. I stood there watching her shallow breathing until she opened her eyes and attempted to follow a light that was shining above my head, moving them back and forth as if trying to follow the light of the sun. But no sunlight had entered the room because the window was closed. My bafflement ended as quickly as it had begun because her eyes quickly rolled back before closing again.

"*¿Como tú andas?*" How are you? I kept asking, until her eyes opened at last to focus on me, as if the unknown light had vanished from her sight. I kept repeating my question until she finally replied, "*Ay, mi hijo.*" Oh, my son. She kept crying the same thing again and again, while faintly squeezing my hand.

I continued repeating myself until La Doña walked into the room. Her swollen eyes were bright red. We both stayed on each side of the bed, assuring Mother that she was safe, encouraging her to breathe, while trying to ignore the sallowness of her face. We stayed for hours, until the doctor finally came in and asked that I step into the hallway so he could speak to me.

"*Mire, casi la perdimos pues empezó a sangrar en el medio de la noche, pero yo creo que ella ya ahora está bien. Su histerectomía fue una operación muy difícil*". Look, we almost lost her, he explained, because she started bleeding in the middle of the night. But I believe she is fine now. Her hysterectomy was a difficult operation.

I stopped breathing as the ward started to spin. I saw myself standing in the delivery room watching my birth, staring at the gleaming forceps creating the dent on the side of my head, watching Mother's blood engulfing my bare feet until I felt its stickiness and choked on its metallic taste, seeing my own lifeless blue self with cord marks around my neck.

Then the world turned pitch black as I fell limp, only to be held up by a nurse who guided me to the floor as she yelled out for help. I could hear her asking me to open my eyes, but they must have been open because I saw the Milky Way stars rapidly pass by me and through me. I could hear crickets and frogs. I could smell Mamá's hot chocolate waiting at the kitchen table for me. I could sense Abuela's presence in the distant light, repeatedly telling me to listen to the nurse. Then Abuela and the light and the stars faded away until I was back on the floor, with my head resting on her lap. It was as if Abuela and the stars had somehow unlocked the sacred knowledge I'd searched for all of my life.

"*¿Fue mi culpa?*" Had it been my fault? That was all I could ask as I opened my eyes.

I stayed there in the nurse's arms as she continued to explain that the damage during my birth hadn't been the cause for the situation Mother was in. I stayed there until help came in the form of a nun, and together, the two women got me back on my feet and helped me into her room. Mother was still asleep, and I sat on a chair next her.

⟨∾⟩

I felt as if I, too, had been sent back from my own bleeding death and given a command to forgive her at last, because I had seen what her life had been. I still couldn't find it within me to show her any kindness, because stepping away from that guarding space, where I'd always lived was too frightening. I didn't know how to replace my anger with affection. This was something that I'd ever witnessed.

I alone had raised myself in a family that showed care by displaying their honorable deeds for all to see. I never saw the emotions behind all of those worldly things. I may have been well-clothed and fed, but when did Mother, Father, Tía Cecilia, or even Mamá, ever show true affection to me?

I could dutifully brush Mother's hair and help her walk up and down the hall as a demonstration of affection for the world to see. After all, I knew how to display what everyone wanted me to be. No one needed to know about the void I didn't know how to fill, and I wondered if that wasn't the same void that Mother had spent all her life trying to fill?

No, I could never be happy simply becoming one of them, because I had changed from a child into a young man who had experienced too much. I knew that allowing myself to live within their emptiness would one day return me to another night of yellow-pill shivering.

Who were my role models, then? Had Abuela not always shown me what affection should be? Had Joaquín, Pilar, and even Don Pepe and Doña Lucia, not shown me what a loving family could be?

⟨∾⟩

These revelations were my act of atonement, my reward. This was God's hand acting through me. Yes, I was good, and held the power to be good. Yes, I was ready to walk away from the mistakes of my past.

I'd walked to the River Styx, paid the ferryman, stepped into Hades, and been allowed to return. Never again would I allow myself to step to the doors of hell.

DESTINY

Two months had passed since Mother returned home from her surgery and went back to working at the apartment's dining room beauty shop where Doña Catalina knitted and fanned her heart. In many ways, life remained unchanged.

But I had changed. My mind was clear and focused, at last. I understood that Mother needed to be with her own kind to rebuild a life independent from me. And I understood that if I were to ever be free to live my own life, she needed to build a life no longer consumed by controlling me or worrying about me. Methodically, I reached out to all her cousins in the States because I knew our time to leave Spain would soon come. I had to find a place for her, and in the short term, for me.

Many answers came, and I shared the responses with her. I even helped her see that staying with her cousin Marta in a New Jersey town called Union City was the best decision to make.

I held back that I wanted to live across the river from the great metropolis of New York. I didn't tell her about Joaquín's plans to apply for medical school in the States, or that New York City seemed like the most logical place for achieving such a thing. Why move to California, as Mother wanted to do, when Madrid was only a non-stop flight away from New York?

I had imagined a future with him attending medical school and me studying to become a nurse so I could help hurting people, just as the nurse at the charity ward had helped me. That nurse holding me in her lap and assuring me that Mother's injuries were not my fault had allowed me to imagine a totally different world where I was no longer to blame.

I wanted to spend my life helping others, with Joaquín next to me. I'd found a purpose, and I had a goal. I'd found a way to share the value of my life.

Our journey day came in late February of 1971, as a seventeenth birthday gift to me, two years after arriving in Madrid. Despite the joyful news, sadness and loss lingered nearby as I faced walking away from Anita and Mariana, and even Doña Catalina's comical fan.

The revolution had forged a world where strangers quickly came together in their shared adversity, built intense emotional bonds to survive, then just as quickly forced them to move on and reinvent their lives once more. I hadn't understood this, until then. This had been the revolution's greatest curse: turning the Cuban people into a band of itinerant vagabonds.

The evening before our departure, as Anita, Mariana, and I sat at the dining table, holding hands, none of us knew if we would ever be together again.

That night, as I sat on that folding cot for the last time, as I stared at the shadows brought to life by the dim light of my lamp—I was consumed by premonitions I couldn't understand.

Mother and Pilar sat in the back of Joaquín's little black car, and I sat in the front seat next to him. Joaquín and I were happy because of our plans. As for Mother, she seemed to exist inside some magical dream, almost unaware of what was taking place. Was she secretly dreaming of Valentín?

Only Pilar seemed sad, because she knew that her brother's plans for school in the States would one day separate her from him.

Barajas Airport, with its shiny wide halls, was as it had always been. Everything seemed as familiar as the day of our arrival in Spain. Yet so much had happened in those many months. I was no longer a confused child who'd woven dreams from spun sugar and meringue. I had become a responsible young man with love and kindness in his heart.

Waiting for the flight to board, Joaquín, Pilar, and I held each other in a tight circle until the first announcement came. Then she pulled away to let him and me embrace with an affectionate public kiss. There—now the entire world knew.

"No te olvides de mí, mi amor." Never forget about me, my love, he said.

"Nunca," Never, I replied, as I let go of his hand, then turned around and walked away with Mother next to me. She seemed weak. Her skin glowed with a rare yellow tinge.

I turned back only once to see Pilar holding onto Joaquín as tears flowed from his eyes. I didn't cry. I pushed ahead in defiant eagerness because I knew who I was, and understood that life could be whatever I wanted it to be. I was no longer afraid for Joaquín because we had made excellent plans. We knew that our life in the States would offer us a future filled with infinite opportunities.

Waiting for us on the runway, I didn't see a sleek Iberia DC-8, with its swept-back wings and slender engines leaping forward like a gazelle. Rather, I saw a stout TWA 707, with its fat engines standing to attention like a general reviewing his troops. The sky was clear, and the sun felt warm against my face. There was no breeze. For a second, I heard a Russian communist march, but it faded away when I remembered that I wasn't in Cuba. America—not the revolution—waited for me. I told myself that Castro and the revolution could never harm me again.

The crowd and the mood on board was quite different from our Iberia flight to Spain, because it felt as if we were attending a great social gathering. People wouldn't stay in their seats. Instead they ran up and down the aisles like children playing a game. The games continued until the meat loaf and apple pie meal was served, and we all settled down to watch a spy movie about Cuba, which somehow confirmed for us all that leaving our beautiful island had been the right decision.

As I looked at the silver sky above the clouds, through the window on my right, my mind drifted away from the flickering on the small screen to build a cocoon where I could think about what lay ahead and what remained behind.

I wanted to receive a divine sign telling me that everything would turn out well for Mother, as well as for Joaquín and me. I wanted to push my mind forward in time, but no miracle revealed itself to me. It didn't matter, I decided, for I held the power of hope and determination in my hands.

Our landing at New York's JFK Airport brought thankful prayers of salvation which rolled back and forth throughout the cabin like waves: *"¡Ay Bendito!" "¡Gracias, Señor!" "¡Santa Maria!"* Oh, blessed one! Thank you, Lord! Holy Mary!

These prayers continued until the plane had come to a stop and the doors were opened, at last. Then chaos took over as the passengers fought to be the first to disembark. But not me. I wanted to be the last one to get up from my seat and leave. I wanted to take my time standing at the top of the staircase, just as I had dared to do on the day when I left my beautiful homeland.

❧

I stood atop the platform, welcoming the sunlight reflecting against the snowy tarmac's edge, and allowed myself, at last, to accept the sadness of my childhood, which I had always worked so hard to reject.

I understood then that I couldn't have been at fault for all that had happened. I was a child—a virgin lump of clay to be molded by Mother's emotions, Father's detachment, Miguel's betrayal, Sebastián's self-hatred, Fernando's act of rape, and by all the unshaved men and their lust.

A breeze, soft with the scent of rosewater, caressed my face and I felt Abuela's kiss on my cheek. She was with me. She gave me strength. My soul finally lived in the present. I was liberated at last.

I inhaled my first American breath, followed by another and another until my lungs were full and the oxygen in my blood had been exchanged.

I took my first step down before reaching back to let Mother take my hand.

ACKNOWLEDGMENTS

I didn't write this novel alone. I was guided and nurtured along the way by innumerable individuals, family, and friends.

I offer my gratitude to Valley Haggard and her amazing Life in 10 classes, for making me believe that I was a writer and a storyteller.

To Elizabeth Ferris, who was the first to review my scribblings and story outline, and who showed me the possibilities.

To Amy Ritchie Johnson, the talented and critical teacher who pushed me to work harder and move beyond pretty superficialities.

To all my writing classmates and friends who encouraged me throughout this journey.

To Mary Jo McLaughlin, a talented writer, author, and dear friend. Thank you for all the clarity and humanity you brought into my work.

To my darling Jer, for celebrating the good times with me and holding me when I was at my worst.

To Elizabeth Turnbull at Light Messages Publishing, who heard the music I heard and understood the poetry in my heart.

To Mary, Tracey, Donnie, Kai, and Jessie for taking the long journey with me.

To my father, for trying to remain engaged despite his own limitations, even during the moments when I refused to acknowledge him.

To my mother, whose death was like a whisper rather than a cry filled with turmoil and regret. Thank you for teaching me to never give up.

To everyone I have ever known, for we are all but one universal human family and part of a most extraordinary world.

ABOUT THE AUTHOR

For as long as he can remember Lorenzo Chavez has been an observer, an explorer, and a storyteller.

As a young boy inspired by old Hollywood movies such as *Robin Hood* or *Prince Valiant*, he penned extraordinary tales of heroes rescuing loved ones in distress. But most of all, he cherished writing about the summers at his maternal grandparents' farm where no one bullied him, and no man desired him. Alone there, surrounded by Cuba's beautiful countryside, away from the chaos of his Havana home, he would discover his perseverance and strength.

He arrived in New York City at seventeen after a two-year exile in Spain without any money, not knowing the language, and lacking the skills to step into a world unlike anything that he had ever known. Against a mountain of obstacles, Lorenzo found a way to make his new country home, attend college, and build a professional and personal life for himself.

Today, he lives in Virginia, USA, with his husband of over twenty-five years and a spirited Corgi Mix named Lucy Honeychurch in honor of E. M. Forster's protagonist in *A Room with a View*.